THE WOMAN IN THE ATTIC

A.J. RIVERS

The Woman in the Attic

Copyright © 2024 by A.J. Rivers

All rights reserved. Without limiting the rights under copyright reserved above, no part of this publication may be reproduced, stored in or introduced into retrieval system, or transmitted, in any form, or by any means (electronic, mechanical, photocopying, recording, or otherwise) without the prior written permission of both the copyright owner and the above publisher of this book.

This is a work of fiction. Names, characters, places, brands, media, and incidents are either the products of the author's imagination or are used fictitiously. The author acknowledges the trademarked status and trademark owners of various products referenced in this work of fiction, which have been used without permission. The publication/use of these trademarks is not authorized, associated with, or sponsored by the trademark owners.

PROLOGUE

T HEY SHOULD HAVE LISTENED TO THE RAIN.
It tried to warn them with tumultuous clouds that hung at the edges of a darkening sky. The weather was predicted to be clear throughout the night. So, they didn't heed the foreboding signs.

The deeper the boys moved into the woods, the darker the sky grew. The clouds pressed in until they blotted out the stars and filtered the moonlight like layers of gauze.

It was only the two of them out there. Maybe if there had been others, someone would have felt the shift in the air and the impending pressure of the rain.

They had come into the woods on a dare. They'd heard stories of the house hidden deep within the trees beyond where good sense existed. The legend diverged on the history of the house. One version claimed the house had been there longer than anyone could remember.

The other alleged the house had appeared spontaneously one day, just appeared there without human effort.

They didn't believe either, of course. They knew the truth lay somewhere in between. But it didn't really matter to Tyler or Gary. They just wanted to know what was inside.

There was no shortage of stories about the house and what was beyond the fence that blocked it away from the rest of the woods. The two boys had talked themselves into a fervor over it, goading each other until there was nothing else they could do but decide to go inside and face it for themselves. They said they didn't believe in ghosts. They told each other they weren't afraid. They were lying.

They'd both seen the house before, so they knew it really did exist. It was only a small glimpse while they were exploring the dense trees with other friends, just enough that they were able to confirm that the actual existence of the house wasn't just a story. They'd seen the fence overgrown with ivy and young trees trying to reclaim the property. That's when the stories started bubbling up among them. The other guys there with them that day told their own, swearing every single word to be true even though the next time they told a story that they heard from someone else, it was totally different.

Maybe they were all true. Maybe the house was filled with ghosts while also being the home base for an evil coven and the home of a cannibal. Maybe it really was built on a burial ground and also used cursed wood because it was stolen from a church and the stones on the face were pieces of tombstones from cemeteries that had been paved over.

And maybe none of it was true. Maybe it was just an empty house that used to belong to a family that died out and left it out there.

But that wasn't very exciting. That didn't get their adrenaline pulsing, give them something they felt would boost their reputations, and get them the attention of the girls who barely looked their way in the hallways. Once they heard that Tyler and Gary went inside the house and brought back pictures to prove it, everyone would look at them differently, and they would be like kings. They each already knew which girls they had their eyes on. They already knew which of the effortlessly popular guys they were going to show the pictures to as they told the tale nonchalantly as if this wasn't affecting them at all.

It was affecting both of them. They didn't want to show it because if they showed it, then it would be real, and they would actually have to deal with it rather than just shoving it down as hard as they could and pretending it didn't exist so they could just keep putting one foot in front of the other.

They should have listened to the rain.

It had started to fall lightly when they were walking through the woods, feeling like they had either gone too far or in the wrong direction because they hadn't come on it yet. It was falling even harder when they finally reoriented themselves and realized they were going in the right direction. By the time they caught a glimpse of the house blotting out what little moonlight existed, raindrops stung their eyes. They got closer and saw the fence surrounding the house. There had to be a gate somewhere, but neither of them knew exactly where it was.

"How do we get inside?" Tyler asked.

"We could climb over the fence," Gary suggested

But as they got closer, they noticed coils of barbed wire along the top of the metal fence and changed their minds about attempting the leap. Instead, they walked along the perimeter, shining their flashlights on the fence until they finally found a section lifted out of the ground. It looked like it might have been cut with wire cutters at some point. It wasn't a large section that could be picked up and held for them to climb through, but it was enough to force their way to the other side.

Gary grunted as the sharp points of the wire scraped along the back of his neck. They caught the small backpack he was wearing, making it feel like somebody had grabbed hold of him and was trying to yank him back away from the house. He almost shouted before he realized what was happening. Tyler helped him disentangle the backpack, and they pushed the rest of the way onto the property itself.

They both tried to let out sighs of relief when they stood and realized they'd made it through without anything stopping them, but the breath stayed stuck in the center of their chests. They'd only gotten so far as the overgrown, weed-matted lawn. A cracked back patio was still several yards ahead, and beyond it, the house itself.

With nothing else they could use to delay what they came to do, they followed the beams of their flashlights across what was likely once beautiful landscaping fit into the wooded surroundings that were probably not as thick when the house was built.

Tyler stopped suddenly, his eyes darting to the side to chase something he thought he saw in the corner of one. It was just a flicker, a glisten in the darkness, but it shouldn't have been there. It was far too bright to be the rain-dulled moon or one of the stars strangled by the thick clouds overhead. The only light that bright should have been one of their flashlights, but they were both shining onto the ground in front of them to make sure they didn't fall, and he thought he saw it up on the house itself.

"Wait," he said,

"What's wrong?" Gary asked. There was a hint of something close to relief in his voice. Like he thought he would not be the one that would stop them from going inside.

Until that point, it had been a game of chicken deciding who was going to make the decision that he'd taken a couple of steps too many and wasn't as interested as he thought he was in telling a story and showing off pictures. No one ever had to know. It wasn't like they told anyone they were coming. That would have come off as too desperate. Doing it this way meant they could act like the entire thing was no big deal and they just came on the idea on a whim.

It meant if they didn't go any further, if they just followed their flashlights back across the old lawn and through the break in the fence, went back through the woods and got into the car, soaked and cold but fully intact, they could just go back to Gary's house. They could spend the rest of the night playing video games and gradually forgetting this ever seemed like a good idea.

Tyler lifted his hand toward what he thought was the flicker of light.

"I thought I saw a light on in the house," he said.

Gary looked toward where he was pointing, searching for any sign of what Tyler was trying to point out to him.

"There wouldn't still be electricity out here, would there?" he asked.

"Even if there was, who would have turned it on?" Tyler asked.

Gary shook his head. "You must have seen a reflection. I don't see anything now."

Tyler had to admit he saw nothing in the dark house now that he looked at it more closely, but he couldn't escape the nagging feeling that he had seen it. A glow somewhere in one of the windows. Maybe not enough to light up an entire room, but enough to be a lamp or a lantern.

They got onto the patio and looked at the dilapidated old furniture scattered across the cement by years and weather. A massive pot, cracked along one side and spilling out dirt and roots, held a tree that seemed to be thriving just fine now that it had broken through the pottery.

"How do we get inside?" Gary asked, looking around for any obvious point of entry that would make it easy for them.

"Try the door," Tyler said, gesturing with his flashlight to the double doors leading out into the house from the patio.

As he was saying it, he already knew they were going to be locked, but they were the only option he could see. The handles on both doors didn't budge when the boys tried to push them.

"Any other ideas?" Gary asked, the rain pouring down on him and the chill along his back quickly taking away any novelty this might have had. Even the fear and uneasiness were starting to fade beneath his discomfort and frustration.

They walked around the patio and looked at the house. It wasn't just a dark shell now that they were up close. They could see details in the architecture—a strange, dark beauty that brought on a different kind of chill.

After waiting for a few seconds, Gary decided he wasn't going to wait for Tyler to come up with something else. He strode across the patio and picked up a piece of broken-off cement. Walking up to one of the large windows to the side of the doors, he threw the chunk of stone. The window shattered under the impact, and Gary kicked away the rest of the glass. He paused and listened, not sure for what, but feeling like he needed that breath.

When he didn't hear anything, he gestured at the window.

"We're in."

"Go ahead," Tyler said.

There was no more time to keep stretching out. Nothing left to keep them from proving to themselves that they could face whatever was inside the house.

Gary climbed through the window first, careful not to catch any of the broken glass still clinging to the frame. Rather than turning his back on whatever lay beyond, he took a step to the side and shone his flashlight to help guide Tyler inside.

"What now?" he asked as his feet crunched on the broken glass scattered across the floor.

Gary shook the raindrops off, debating whether he was glad for the shelter or if he would rather still be out in the rain.

"We look around. That's what we came here for, isn't it?" he snapped.

It looked like they'd broken into a sunroom, but there was no furniture. They continued and entered a living room. A few pieces of furniture remained, draped in cloth like burial shrouds. A haunting painting of a woman hung on the wall, the features all but obliterated with a thick layer of dust and cobwebs. The house felt cavernous and confusing now that they were inside. With no idea of the layout or what they might find, they could only wander around, waiting for doors to open to more inky-black spaces.

"Hold on," Tyler whispered into the still, musty darkness. "Did you hear that?"

"Hear what?" Gary asked.

"That sound. I thought I heard something."

They paused and listened. Silence stretched in all directions.

"I don't hear any—"

The sound of something shifting against the floor stopped Gary in the middle of his sentence.

"Holy shit, what was that?"

The sound came again, a little louder this time. It was something close to footsteps, but not as loud as they would expect. They drew in closer to each other, turning so their backs were nearly pressed to each other as they moved the beams of their flashlights throughout the room where they were standing.

Both were listening for the sound to come again and hoping it wouldn't. When several seconds passed and it didn't, Tyler took a slight step away from Gary.

"It was probably an animal," he said. "I doubt that window we broke is the only way into this place for something small."

His flashlight shone on the wall, and he noticed an old light switch on the peeling, faded floral wallpaper. On a whim, he walked up to it and flicked the switch. It did nothing. Seeing the light coming from the house really did have to be a reflection or just a fleeting moment of imagination.

They moved deeper into the house and started snapping pictures of the things they were seeing. Neither heard the low humming sound under the pounding of the rain.

"Let's go to the basement and get a couple pictures there, go up to the bedroom, then get the hell out of here," Gary suggested.

By then, they had captured images of at least most of the parts of the house that appeared in the stories they heard. The basement and an upstairs bedroom were all that were left so they could dispel all the myths hovering over the house.

They searched until they found a door in the kitchen and opened it. A blast of cold air came up to them, along with a scent that was distinctly metallic. It didn't have the same dank quality as the rest of the house, but it struck them almost like the smell of the cold. They walked down the step cautiously, debating whether to close the door behind them as they went or if they should leave it open. It was still open as they made their way along the creaking planks of wood toward the cement pad at the bottom, illuminated by Tyler's flashlight.

"What in the living fuck?" Gary suddenly asked.

Tyler had been concentrating so much on not falling down the steps that he hadn't taken his eyes off them. He didn't see what Gary was seeing as he swung his own flashlight back and forth into the open basement space. Tyler looked up, and his stomach dropped.

The basement wasn't the dingy, dirty space he'd expected it to be, lined with shelves heavy with old canned goods and relics of a past era. Instead, he saw a smooth, polished floor and a large metal table. Adding his flashlight beam to Gary's, they illuminated several large, white chest freezers positioned along the walls. They reached the bottom of the steps and looked around, trying to make sense of what they were seeing. From down in the basement, they could hear the hum of a generator that must have been hidden outside, somewhere they weren't able to see as they approached the house.

There were six massive freezers, along with large metal cabinets set in between. The smell of the cold now held a tinge of something sharp and chemical.

"Open one of them," Gary told Tyler.

"Why should I?" Tyler asked. "You open it."

"We'll go together," he said.

They gingerly approached one of the freezers and started to lift the latch on the front. Before they could open it, light suddenly flooded the room, and footsteps started down the stairs. They were unmistakable this time. The boys panicked, realizing there was no other way to get out of the room that they had noticed.

They didn't have time to search for another door. They didn't even process the figure that came down the steps toward them. They could only think about running. Both extended their arms as they went, pushing the person clothed in a heavy raincoat out of the way so they stumbled and fell to the ground.

Neither one of the boys listened for the sound of the person coming behind them. They didn't want to know if they were being pursued. All they cared about was getting out of the house. From their earlier exploration, they knew how to get to the front door. It was closer and an easier way to get out of there than trying to climb back through the window they'd broken. Fumbling with the locks on the door with shaking hands, they finally succeeded and threw the door wide open so they could run out. Not bothering to close it behind them, they ran across a sagging wooden front porch and down creaking steps.

As they ran, they noticed something strange at the front of the house. They wouldn't process what it was until later. They were far too focused on running across the lawn and risking the barbed wire by jumping over the fence. Torn clothes and a couple of scratches were well worth the feeling of the forest floor beneath their feet and the darkness of the trees pressing in around them again.

They ran until they couldn't anymore.

CHAPTER ONE

"I DON'T EVEN KNOW HOW TO EXPLAIN IT," I SAY, PICKING UP the bowl of tortilla chips and a container of guacamole to bring out into the backyard. "It was just one of the eeriest interactions I've ever had. He was perfectly calm and said nothing that was really suspicious on the surface, but it felt completely off. It was like that movie with the burlap guy when they pull the string and inside is a bunch of bugs. That kind of feeling."

"To be fair," Xavier says, following behind me with a plate of taco shells and a bowl of seasoned meat, "having an interaction with a man comprised of burlap wouldn't be the most reassuring experience. I think I would know something wasn't right."

"He speaks the truth," Emma says from in front of me.

She has already brought out salsa, lettuce, diced tomatoes, and shredded cheese. Sam is still in the kitchen negotiating how to bring out beans, rice, roasted corn, and a pitcher of iced tea to go with the water already sitting on the table in the backyard.

I'm telling them more details about my strange conversation with the member of the Board from Twilight Cove when I was investigating the murders of Joseph Palmer and Scott Russo during Mardi Gras. I don't know exactly how to get it across to them just how odd the conversation was. It wasn't so much what was said, but it was the energy coming off the man who came out of the back of the sprawling headquarters as if to represent the entire mysterious organization.

"I feel like I have so many more questions now than I even did before I knew who killed them. I know Seth did it, but why?"

"I thought you said it had something to do with one of his friends," Emma says.

"No, I know that. But I still don't understand what kind of secret Palmer could have been preparing to talk about with Russo that was so intense that the Board would have him killed for it," I say.

"But you still can't be completely sure this Board actually had anything to do with it," Sam says. "You made that connection with Seth, but you couldn't prove that they sent him after Palmer and Russo."

"And that's only making it worse," I point out. "Because I know they had something to do with it. I know they sent Seth after those two because of a secret that they were going to expose on Russo's podcast. They just knew how to cover their tracks and make sure that no one was able to follow what they were doing."

The case involving the content producer was complicated and dizzying when I was digging into it alongside Detective Peter Bronson from the Echo Harbor Police Department. Shared across the small communities of Echo Harbor and Twilight Cove, the police department was spread thin by a flurry of crimes surrounding the holiday, and I found myself involved in the murder investigation after being hired on a completely unrelated case. Though I was able to prove the identity of the killer, his own murder before we were able to apprehend him—along with the heavy cloud of questions still hanging over me—means the Joseph Palmer and Scott Russo case is still an open wound for me. I will not stop until I find out why he was being tormented the way he was and what he was holding on to that was enough to kill.

"You haven't gotten any closer to figuring out what his secret was?" Emma asks as we sit down in the cool early summer evening air to eat dinner.

To one side, a blanket spread across the grass holds an assortment of Xavier's newest sourdough babies, also enjoying some fresh air. He recently went on a tear, dehydrating much of his collection, so the number of jars he grapples with has been greatly diminished. But now his storage room is filled with neatly lined up containers of the powder, labeled with their names and the types of flour used to make them. Fortunately, he's also been on a baking rampage recently, especially when Cupcake comes to spend time with him. So much of the discard is being used, and not as many babies are being given their own jars and occasional tiny accessories. Today's addition of "What's Loaves Got to Do With It" is the first in a while.

The pendulum will swing in the other direction soon, and he'll start building up the collection more rapidly again. The summer weather doesn't really cry out for a lot of time with the oven on or copious loaves of bread, trays of biscuits, and containers of crackers filling the kitchen. Come fall again, though, the kitchen will be alive with the sound of baking, and everyone who exists anywhere near the family is going to end up with some kind of baked good.

"I have no idea," I tell her. "I thought there might be something in his files, but it looks like he destroyed everything that could have contained what he was hiding. He was trying to protect the people at the party by doing what he was told, but I don't think it actually mattered. I think he would have been killed no matter what."

"They were just toying with him," Emma says, her voice solemn.

I know she's thinking about her own extremely complex and haunting case now. There were similarities at the beginning of her investigation into the horrific killing of a church leader, enough that we briefly considered the idea that they might be related in some way. The heaviness in her voice and the chill behind the words are palpable as the statement settles over the table.

"Did you know that the word *taco* is only from the eighteenth century and originated from silver miners in Mexico?" Xavier suddenly asks to fill the silence.

It's enough to detour the conversation and get us talking about other things, but a piece of my mind is still stuck on the lingering questions in Twilight Cove.

We're cleaning up from dinner and getting the firepit, which I recently added to the backyard, ready to toast some marshmallows when my phone rings. I'm surprised to see my friend Kent's name on the screen.

"Hey, Kent," I answer. "How's it going?"

"Great," he says. "I hope it's not too late to call."

"Of course not," I say. "Xavier and I are just hanging out with my cousin Emma and her husband, Sam."

"Then I won't take up a lot of your time," he says. "I just wanted to call and let you know that Sylvia and I have finally gotten settled into our new house."

"That's fantastic," I say.

The couple, whom I've known for many years since my time in the service, went through a rough time for a while and ended up having to leave the home they'd been in for years, but finally, they found a house they loved. Everything fell into place perfectly, and I knew they'd be moving in soon, so it's great to hear that they had finalized everything and finally managed to get settled in.

"I was hoping that I could still take you up on that offer to come and help us out with a few repairs and improvements," he says. There's a cautious tinge to his voice, like he's almost embarrassed to be making the call.

He shouldn't be. I was the one who made the offer when he first told me they found a house they loved but that there were a few things about it that were going to need attention when they finally got the chance to move in.

"I wouldn't have made the offer if I didn't want you to take me up on it," I tell him. "I can come up there this weekend if that works for you."

"That would be amazing. Thank you. I really appreciate your help," he says.

"No problem. It'll be good to hang out."

"Bring Xavier along too if he wants to come," Kent says.

"I'll ask him. Thanks. Send me the address, and let me know if there are any tools or anything you need me to bring with me," I say. "I'll see you soon."

I hang up and go back outside to where the others are fully invested in getting the perfect crispy caramel coating on the outside of their marshmallows. Except for Xavier, who only accepts toasted marshmallows if they are set ablaze before being taken out of the fire. If we get the jumbo variety of marshmallows, he likes to peel off the charred outside and eat it, then put the rest back into the fire for another go-round.

"New client?" Emma asks as I pick up a fork and skewer a marshmallow with it before sitting down beside the fire.

"No," I tell her. "That was my old buddy Kent Carruthers. He and his wife, Sylvia, just moved into a new house, and I offered to help them do some projects. I'm going to go over there this weekend and see what I can help them with."

"Where's the new house?" Emma asks.

THE WOMAN IN THE ATTIC

"Briar Glen," I tell her. I look over at Xavier. "They said to bring you along too, X."

"I can't. Nicole is coming over to the Harlan house this weekend to help go through some things and see what we might be able to donate or get rid of so we can start getting it ready," he tells me.

The process of building a house out on the farmland that Xavier bought is still very much in its infancy, with only the most basic steps having been taken and him still making decisions about the design, but the process of getting the Harlan house ready to sell is far more daunting. It means Xavier is going to have to go through years of possessions, inventions, gadgets, storage, and memories and figure out what is going to go to the new house and what isn't. For other people, that might take a couple of weeks. It is a far more strenuous task for Xavier, so he's starting it now when he knows he has months to work gradually on the task.

I'm actually really proud of him for what he's accomplished so far. Just the fact that he's planning the move is already fairly monumental. Xavier does not like change. He does not like the unfamiliar. The house in Harlan has been his home for decades, remaining there waiting for him even during the years he was in prison. It contains everything that was his life during his early adult years and on through his struggles, discoveries, and triumphs, then the horrors of Andrew's murder and the challenging climb back out into the world.

Even when we started spending more time in Sherwood to be close to Emma and Sam, I thought that house would always belong to Xavier and he would gravitate back to it every so often just to be in the space that was so comfortable and familiar to him. But he made the decision completely on his own, and without even talking to me about it, to not only buy the farm property but also to put everything that the house represented behind him and move on to a new chapter in his life.

Since I can get clients wherever I go and the reputation I've built up on my own as well as by working with Emma on her cases has me traveling to my cases more often than not, it doesn't really matter where I call home. But the move does feel like major things are shifting, and I wonder what else could change.

"I'm sorry I won't be around to help you," I say.

"It's all right. You know how Nicole is. She'll make sure everything is under control. She doesn't have any parties planned for this weekend, so all her attention is going into the storage room at the top of the steps," he says.

That could mean one of several locations in the house, but any of them would be a tremendous amount of work, so I'm appreciative of the bold, dynamic woman who found her way into our lives by advertising herself as a pet sitter. She's been good for Xavier, and I know she'll help him with the hard decisions that are going to come as he's going through the house.

As Emma and Sam leave for their house a couple of streets away, I think about what I need to do to get ready for the weekend in Briar Glen with Kent and Sylvia. I'm glad he called. I'm looking forward to seeing him after a long time of only communicating through texts and the occasional phone call. But I also know that concentrating on something like doing repairs and improvements around their house will be good for me. It will help break me out of my cyclical thoughts about Palmer, Russo, and the Board.

CHAPTER TWO

I HELP XAVIER CARRY THE JARS OF SOURDOUGH STARTER BACK INTO the house. We take them to the spare bedroom that has become their home when we aren't in the Harlan house, where they live in the converted parlor behind the kitchen.

"Thank you, Dean," he says as I settle the last of the jars onto one of the shelves in the center of the room.

"You're welcome," I say. "I think they look comfortable."

"No. Thank you," he says.

I look at him questioningly. "For what?"

"Everything. Thank you for everything you've done for me since that judge chose you as my guardian. I don't know if I've ever actually thanked you for doing that," he says.

I'm surprised at the sudden change of conversation, unsure of why it's come up now.

"You have," I tell him.

"I've thanked you for things, but I really want you to know that I appreciate what you did for me all those years ago. You weren't standing in that courtroom waiting for the judge to tell you that you were going to be the one to watch out for me and make sure that I functioned..."

"Xavier..."

"No, listen," he says, cutting me off from stopping him. "You don't need to pretend like you don't know why the judge decided I needed someone. You don't have to try to preserve my feelings or act like you don't know exactly why she would be concerned just releasing me out into the public after nearly a decade in custody. That's not going to do either of us any good. The ugly duckling might have become a beautiful swan, but that doesn't erase a lifetime of social ostracization and mockery because of his innate biological inability to fully assimilate to the surroundings foisted on him by the belief that he had to be a duck."

"Um..."

"I just want you to know that I understand it wasn't something you wanted or would have chosen for yourself, and I appreciate that you did it. I appreciate all the time I've had with you," he says. "And everything you've done for me and helped me to be able to do for myself."

"X, that judge might have decided I needed to be the one to help you in that second, but I cared about you even then. If I had known they were going to have someone else do it, I would have stepped in and offered," I say. "But the most important thing is that the judge chose us for each other right then, out of necessity. I completely understand that. I'm not going to pretend like I don't see the challenges that you go through and that I don't realize your struggles were far worse then than they are now. You needed somebody to help you figure out the world that had passed you by, and the judge wanted to make sure that you would still be around if they decided to put you through another trial period. I get that. It's not something I like to think about, but I do understand the reason.

"What matters is that whatever was going through that judge's head isn't the reason that I'm standing here right now. I'm still here because I choose to be. That judge chose us for each other at first, but the most important thing to me is that we've chosen to stay together. I can't imagine not having you in my life."

"That's not really an option, Dean," he says flatly, as if there truly isn't a scenario in the realm of possibility where the two of us aren't the way we are.

"Things are changing, X," I tell him. "And that's not necessarily a bad thing."

THE WOMAN IN THE ATTIC

He knows I'm talking about his relationship with Cupcake. I can see in his eyes that it's affecting him. He cares about her. After what he told me about the girl he loved when he was a teenager and the kiss he gave Cupcake so unexpectedly, there's no denying or even questioning it anymore. Something has grown between the two of them, and as much as it has improved him and given him a happiness I haven't seen in him before, it's also worrying him. Again, he doesn't like change. He doesn't always know how to deal with it or what it's supposed to mean. In this situation, he seems to be teetering between letting himself be happy and wondering what's coming next and stopping it all so that things can stay the way they were.

"They don't have to," he says.

"Yes, they do. And you know that. Life is nothing but change, and you don't have to be afraid of it. I promise I'm not going anywhere. You don't have to choose."

"What if I forget?" he asks.

"Forget what?" I ask.

"Everything that's attached to the house in Harlan. I can't stop thinking about it."

"You don't have to go through with it if you don't want to," I say. "Just because you said it was something you were thinking about doing doesn't mean that the decision is set in stone."

"I know. I want to build on the farm. I want to be closer to Sherwood and be able to really enjoy the land out there. But there's so much in Harlan. What if leaving the house means I lose it all?" he asks.

"You won't," I tell him. "You'll put the things you want to put behind you behind you, and the rest will stay because you carry it with you. Remember what you told me about energy? Places remember you. You leave a piece of your energy behind when you go to a place, and it is always there. That means that the opposite is true too. The energy of places stays with you, even long after you've left. Whatever pieces of that house you want to keep with you, they'll come. You'll still have your memories. And you'll have the chance to make new ones."

"I talked to Cupcake today," he tells me, somehow both staying perfectly on topic and detouring the conversation at the same time.

"What about?" I ask.

"She's been thinking more about moving closer. She might find a place in Cherry Hill or Sherwood," he says.

It will mean that if we are in Sherwood, she will always be around, unless she is traveling for work. That means he would get to spend more time with her. But that single sentence holds a lot of weight. A simple change of inflection illustrates the differing meanings that it could hold. He would have the chance to be with her more, which he would enjoy. But he would also spend more time with her, which might get overwhelming.

"How are you feeling about that?" I ask.

"I'm not sure," he says. "Good, I think."

It's exactly the answer I was expecting, and I sling my arm around his shoulders to walk out of the room with him. He'll work through it. And with all the patience and understanding she has already shown, I know she'll take as much time as both of them need and deal with whatever comes.

Xavier and I travel back to Harlan Friday. Early Saturday morning, I'm in my pajama bottoms in the kitchen making coffee to start fueling myself up for the drive to Kent's when the doorbell rings.

"It's Nicole!" Xavier shouts from the pantry, where he's selecting which of the sourdough babies will be baked into crackers today and which will be headed for dehydration.

"I'll get it," I tell him.

Shuffling to the door, I swing it wide and find Nicole on the front porch, laden with boxes and bags. She looks me up and down.

"Nice outfit," she says. "Bit breezy in the upper region maybe, but I can see what you're going for."

She comes into the house, and I close the door.

"What is all that?" I ask, eyeing everything she's carrying as she heads for the living room so she can put it all down.

"I've come prepared to do battle with the storage room," she says. "I have seen that thing only from the doorway, and I am not even going to begin to try to guess what might be happening up in there. I decided to just bring all my organizational tools and figure it out as I go."

Xavier comes into the room, and Nicole points at him.

"And you should know, I already contacted the Harlan Cares charity organization and let them know we would be by later this afternoon with a big donation for them."

He nods. "I won't let them down."

It was a brilliant if risky move. By contacting the charity, she created an expectation for Xavier. He now knows there are people waiting for him to bring things, which means he actually has to go through what he has stashed away over the years and part with things that could be useful to other people. This is a delicate balancing act for Xavier. He may struggle with people on an individual basis, and when they are gathered together in large groups, they can bother him. But as a general concept, he cares about people and doing what he can for them. He would want to help those in need.

At the same time, parting with things is extremely difficult for him and can cause major bouts of anxiety. Objects tend to take on a sense of personality to him, creating an attachment that makes it very hard for him to simply let go of something.

Knowing that there are people who can benefit from what he gets rid of will make it easier, but if he starts to feel pressured or manipulated, it could seriously backfire. I'm glad it's Nicole handling this task with him. There will be plenty of opportunity for me to dig into the rooms and alcoves of this massive house alongside Xavier, putting aside my nagging hesitation surrounding his sometimes treacherous inventions and gadgets for the greater good of getting the house ready to sell. I'll take on that challenge then.

A couple of hours later, they are deep in their excavation of the storage room when I finish packing for my trip. I only plan on being at Kent and Sylvia's house for a few days, so I just have a duffel bag and my computer with me. I toss them into the car and then say goodbye to Nicole and Xavier. She's staying with him for the next couple of days, so I tell them I'll call regularly to check in and wish them luck on their endeavor before getting in my car and heading off.

I'm about an hour into my drive when my phone rings.

"Hey, Celeste," I answer. "How are you doing?"

After the attack she suffered recently that left her beaten and nearly drowned, I haven't stopped worrying about her. I know the doctors cleared her and she's doing fine, but I hate that she went through what she did. Not the least reason for which being that I know deep in my gut she was attacked because she gave me details about the Board. She revealed the shadowy reputation of the group of powerful men who position themselves as pillars of the community, passionately dedicated to charity and volunteering, but who seem to be able to make things happen. I have no doubt that crossing them is what left her floating in that pool after she talked to me.

"Feeling better," she says. "I called because I just heard something I thought you might find interesting."

"What's that?" I ask.

"Scott Russo's former assistant, Leo Cahill, is not only picking right back up where Russo left off, but he's doing a special presentation on Seth Powers that's going to be live tonight," she says.

"Tonight?" I ask. "Are you serious? That seems a little fast."

"That's what I thought too. It doesn't seem like long enough to have all the facts and information he would need to actually do a special," she says. "But that's what's been going around town."

"I guess he could just talk about the basics of what is already publicly known and then do what Russo apparently used to do and fill the rest of it with coming at the story from different angles and a lot of conjecture," I say.

"I don't know what other angles he could come from. It's been all over the news that Seth Powers murdered both Joseph Palmer and Scott Russo."

"There's still the question of why though," I tell her. "That's not public knowledge. As far as I know, it's not police knowledge either. Detective Bronson and I are still in communication, and he hasn't uncovered any new details yet."

"Are you going to be coming back to Twilight Cove soon?" she asks.

"I probably will. I can't stop thinking about this," I tell her.

"Well, at least I'll get to spend more time with you. I wish it were under different circumstances, but I'll take it."

We chat a little longer about what's going on in our lives before hanging up. It was good to hear from her and know that she's still getting better, but I'm particularly intrigued by Leo already putting up a special edition of the podcast about Seth Powers and the murders he committed. I know from talking to him soon after the murders that the former assistant of true crime podcaster Scott Russo always planned on keeping the podcast going. He'd been doing the behind-the-scenes work for Russo since the beginning and didn't want to lose everything he'd already invested in the project. I'm just surprised it happened so quickly.

CHAPTER THREE

I let Kent know when I was getting close to the house, so he's waiting for me out on the country front porch when I pull into the driveway. It's been a long time since I've had a chance to see him in person, and I'm glad to be here finally. He comes out to the car as I'm getting out and gives me a hug, pounding on my back as he greets me.

"So good to see you, man," he says. "How was the drive?"

"Smooth," I tell him. "No traffic or anything."

Behind him, the door opens, and a small dog comes bounding down the steps and over to us. I crouch down to pet his curly brown fur and get a lick on the hand as a reward.

"This is Cocoa," he tells me. "I guess you could say he's our baby."

"You did good," I joke, petting the pup again before straightening and going for my bags.

"Hi, Dean," Sylvia calls from the front porch. "Good to see you."

"You too," I call up to her as Kent takes my duffel and we head up the steps onto the porch.

"This is one thing I want to work on," Kent tells me as he points out a couple of broken steps and some peeling paint. "I'd also really like to get the porch swing hung."

There's a white porch swing sitting on the wood, its chains pooled around it, just waiting to be hoisted up into position.

"That's easy," I tell him. "We can get that done without a problem."

"Great," he tells me. "Then that leaves all your effort for everything else I'm hoping to get done while you're here."

I laugh and walk through the front door into the house. The air-conditioning feels crisp and refreshing after the damp heat outside, and I pause in the entryway just to enjoy it.

"I'll show you your room," Sylvia says, heading up a flight of stairs.

I follow behind her, and she points out a room to the right of the landing.

"The bathroom is right there," she tells me, pointing out a door beside the closed bedroom door. "You'll have it to yourself. We have one in our room." She gestures to a door on the other side of the hallway.

"Let's drop off your stuff and get you a cold drink," Kent says. "Then I'll finish showing you around."

I go into the room they set aside for me and drop my computer bag onto the bed made up in navy-blue-and-cream bedding. It's positioned across from a window with curtains pulled back to reveal a view of the backyard. Kent follows behind me and sets my duffel beside my computer bag.

"Anything else you need up here?" he asks.

"No, this looks great. Thanks," I say.

"Come on, Sylvia just made some fresh lemonade."

We go down to the kitchen, and Sylvia takes a large pitcher out of the refrigerator. Kent grabs glasses out of the cabinet and fills them with ice so she can pour the drink over it. I take a long sip, savoring the perfect balance of sweet and tart and the cool feeling sweeping through my body, further taking the edge off the heat outside.

Sylvia sets a plate of cookies on the island, but I forego one in favor of continuing to drain my glass. Kent points around the kitchen at a couple of minor things he wants to fix and improve, including painting the cabinets and replacing the faucet on the sink. Sylvia adds that she wants us to fix the garbage disposal and add curtains to the window. Finished with our lemonade, we continue through the house, going over the various projects Kent has in mind for our visit.

"I'm not entirely sure what happened to this wall, but I don't know if I really need the full details," he says after we've gone through the upper levels of the house and made it down to the finished basement.

It's small, half of it behind a door that leads to an unfinished area with storage, the hot water heater, and the washer and dryer, but Kent has made the most of it. A TV hangs from one wall facing a gray sectional with several pillows piled in the corners and handmade blankets tossed over the back. A mini refrigerator is against another wall, along with a table perfect for filling with snacks to watch games or movies.

On the far side of the room is a cabinet with glass shelves. I walk up to it and look at the items displayed on it. All of them are memorabilia from Kent's time in the service. Picking up one of the framed pictures, I look down at the smiling faces of a group of us from one of the rare days off we got to spend together.

"We look like babies, don't we?" he asks, coming up beside me.

"We really do," I say. "I didn't realize I was this old until now."

I laugh as I put the picture back and look at the others, feeling a wave of nostalgia wash over me. A couple of books sit on top of one of the shelves, and I already know what they are before picking them up. The first is the book by Charlie, the romanticized and manipulated account of the horrific months we spent stranded in the woods thinking we'd suffered an accidental plane crash during a training exercise.

"He signed it," Kent says, his voice carrying a kind of sadness that only the people who went through the experience, and the brutal aftermath, can fully understand. "The last time I saw him."

I flip open the cover and see his name across the blue background in sweeping penmanship that reminds me of the heady time of fame and fawning attention he experienced after writing the book. I remember watching the talk shows and news broadcasts he showed up on, telling the story that none of the rest of us wanted to tell. We didn't know the truth then. We didn't know what actually happened until after Charlie's gruesome death broke open secrets long buried but still raw.

Putting the book back on the shelf, I pick up the other. It also has Charlie's name on the front cover, but alongside it is my own. This was meant to be Charlie's second book, the one where he was going to tell the actual story of what happened during that training exercise and over the months we spent in the woods. He'd been tormented by what he'd covered up and wanted to come clean about his involvement in the crash and the tests and experiments we were put through. But he never had the chance to tell it. A bomb ripping through his house stopped him.

I had the opportunity to tell the rest of the story for him. He'd collected notes and research, and I combined that information with my own memories and experiences to finish the book as a final legacy for him. It was one of the most difficult things I've done outside my career, but I'm glad I did it. Writing the book was also what put me on the path of Vance after a Christmas party at his house to woo me and others into participating in a TV project based on the book. Now he's become one of my closest friends.

"Did you read it?" I ask.

"Of course," he says. "It wasn't easy, but I had to read it."

I nod and start to put the book down.

"Will you sign it for me?" he asks.

"Sure."

He finds me a pen, and I sign the inside of the front cover. My signature isn't nearly as artistic and sweeping as Charlie's. For a fleeting moment, I wonder what his would look like now.

"Do you ever miss it?" Kent asks after I put the book back and look at a few more of the items on the shelves.

"Sometimes," I say.

It's a hard question to think about. I thought I was going to spend the rest of my life serving in the military. When I joined, it was to save myself and make up for what I saw as massive mistakes I'd made in my life. I thought that was going to be what I did forever, what was going to define me and be the impact I left on the world. But a grisly leg injury abruptly ended my time and left me wondering what I was going to do moving forward.

That was unimaginably hard to go through. There were times when I felt like I had nothing left. I thought I didn't have anything else to offer and didn't know what kind of life I could possibly have. If I'm being honest, there were times when I didn't know if I would make it through the next day. But now that I'm through it and it is many years behind me, I have a different perspective. It was only because I had to leave the service that I became a private investigator. And it's through the career that I've come to love that I found my family.

I didn't know Emma was my cousin when my investigation first put me on her trail. But now I can't imagine my life without her and Sam. And without them, I wouldn't have Xavier in my life, not to mention all the others who have become such important parts of my existence. I'm happy with where I've ended up and am grateful for everything I have. But there are still times when the pain in my leg brings back a memory, and I find myself longing for that time again.

"How about we grab a couple of beers and get the grill going so we can cook up some hamburgers for supper?" Kent asks.

"That sounds great," I tell him.

He goes to the refrigerator and takes out a couple of bottles of beer. Handing me one, he leads me back up the basement steps and out into the backyard. He opens up the huge grill sitting on his back patio and pours in the charcoal. Lighting it, he shifts the flames around a bit, then comes to sit with me under an umbrella covering a patio table and chairs.

"How's your boy doing?" Kent asks after a few seconds of just relaxing with the refreshing taste of the beer and the summer smell of charcoal heating.

"He's good," I say. "He's been spending a lot of time with his sister, just trying to help her through everything. She kind of shut down after her mother's death, and Owen has been trying to pull her back out of her shell. He's excited about college."

Kent chuckles. "Hard to believe you have a son who is old enough to be going off to college."

I laugh and take a deep swig of my beer. It's especially hard to process, considering what a short time I've had Owen in my life. I missed everything from his childhood and most of his teenage years. But I have him now, and I am doing everything I can to make up for the lost time. We see each other as often as we can. We even went on our first vacation together to celebrate Bellamy and Eric finally getting married. That trip took a gruesome detour that left Emma working far more than relaxing, but I'll still hold on to the memories I was able to make with him.

The next morning, Kent and I are out working on the front porch, but I'm lost in my thoughts as we listen to Leo Cahill's podcast. I suggested it when Kent asked what we should listen to, and he was interested, so we've been listening to Cahill's interpretation of the murders. I was waiting for my name to come up. I didn't tell Kent I was involved in the investigation before we started listening to the podcast, and I figured I would just wait until the mention came to explain it. But the only thing that's been mentioned is a "private investigator."

"Hey, Ron!" Kent calls, breaking me out of my thoughts about the case.

I look up and see Kent waving at a couple across the street. The man is wearing slacks and a shirt and tie, carrying bags out to one of the cars sitting in the driveway. The woman follows behind him with a travel cup.

"Hey, Kent!" the man, who I'm assuming is Ron, calls back.

He puts the bags in the trunk of the car and takes the travel cup from his wife. He leans into the car to put the cup down, then reaches for his wife's hand so the two of them can cross the street toward Kent, who has put down his tools and walked out to the middle of the sidewalk as he wipes his hands. Kent stuffs his bandanna into his back pocket in time to reach for Ron's hand as the other man approaches.

"How're you doing?" Ron asks. "Looks like you're keeping yourself busy."

Kent looks over his shoulder at the progress we've made with the porch.

"Just tackling a few projects around the house. Ron, this is my old friend, Dean Steele. Dean, this is my neighbor Ron McCain and his wife, Erin," Kent says.

"Nice to meet you," I say, shaking their hands.

"You too," Ron says. "I'd offer to help, but I'm leaving for a work conference in South Carolina. It officially starts tomorrow, but I have some boring social obligations with a couple of associates tonight. Then it's a few days of boring work obligations." He chuckles in that warm, almost soothing way that inspires trust and makes you feel like you've known a person for years, even if you've just met them.

I have no idea what Ron McCain does for a living, but as genuine as I feel like he is, I'm sure that chuckle and the strength of his handshake earn him a lot of business, especially if he's in sales of any kind.

"Sounds like a blast," Kent jokes.

"Be sure to keep an eye on Erin for me while I'm gone," he says. "I hate leaving her alone."

He wraps an arm around his wife's waist and gives her a little hug close to his side. Sylvia comes out on the porch and smiles at her neighbors.

"Heading to another conference?" she asks.

Ron nods. "Yep. Hitting the road in just a minute."

"Sylvia, you should come by for coffee sometime this week," Erin says.

"That would be great," Sylvia tells him.

"Well, I've got to get going, but whatever's left to do when I get back, count me in for helping out," Ron says.

"I'll hold you to that," Kent says.

"Dean, nice to meet you."

I nod and wave at them as they make their way back across the street.

"We haven't been here long, but they've been good neighbors. They were the first people to come over and welcome us to the neighborhood. She seriously brought a pie and everything," Kent tells me.

"Sounds like the kind of neighbor you want to have," I say.

"Ready to get back to work?" he asks.

"Let's go."

CHAPTER FOUR

Three days later

S OMETHING WOKE HER UP FROM A DEEP SLEEP. SYLVIA KNEW she was having a dream about something, but it disappeared out of her mind as soon as her eyes opened to a strobing wash of red and white lights coming through her bedroom window. She'd asked Kent to close the blinds before he went to bed, but he'd forgotten. The open wooden slats allowed the flashing lights to pour into the room, making it so she couldn't get comfortable when she closed her eyes to go back to sleep. Kent was curled with his back to the window, so the lights weren't bothering him. Sylvia tried to do the same, but the colors bounced off the cream wall on the side of the room.

Even without the lights reflecting, she didn't think she'd be able to go back to sleep right then. She didn't think it was the lights that woke her up. They were the first thing she noticed when she opened her eyes, but something else broke her out of her sleep. She kept trying to go back to sleep for a few more minutes, then gave up, letting curiosity pull her out of her bed and toward the window. She looked through the blinds and saw an ambulance parked outside of Ron and Erin McCain's house.

She stood watching while an EMT climbed out of the ambulance and headed up to the house. From the distance and past the large tree in her front yard, Sylvia couldn't see any specific features of the person, but she could see that they were carrying a bag of supplies. Concerned, Sylvia got her bathrobe and put it on as she went down the stairs to the dining room. It gave her a better view of the front of the house, and she stood watching, waiting for something to happen.

Several minutes passed before the front door to the house opened. An EMT came out and headed for the back of the ambulance. This person was considerably smaller than the first, telling her it was a second EMT. Like the first, this one was wearing a hat and dark jacket against the cool of the summer predawn. The EMT went to the back of the ambulance and opened the doors, then pulled out a stretcher. They set it up in the street behind the ambulance. Their head suddenly popped up, and they rushed back into the house.

Sylvia watched, waiting breathlessly for a few seconds. She walked out onto the porch and started down the sidewalk, shining the flashlight of her phone in front of her to give her some extra light. She wanted to go across the street and find out what was happening, but when she almost reached the driveway, she heard Kent's voice behind her.

"Babe! What are you doing?" he asked in a loud whisper.

"That ambulance is worrying me," she said. "I want to see what's going on."

"You can't go over there. Whatever's going on, they've got it handled. Come on, it's still really early. We can get a little more sleep. Come back to bed," he said.

Sylvia looked back toward Kent, then at the house again. She was really concerned about Erin. She knew she was home alone now that Ron was gone for his work trip, and she didn't want to think of something bad happening to her while she was by herself. But she also knew that she shouldn't interfere. If there really was something happening, she would just be in the way and distract the emergency responders if she tried to find out any information.

Reluctantly, she turned back around and went inside. They went upstairs to bed, but a few minutes of lying there told her that any chance of her getting any more rest for the night wasn't going to happen. Rolling over, she kissed Kent on the cheek.

"I'm going to get up and take a shower," she said. "Then I'll make some breakfast."

He grunted a response, already almost asleep again. It wasn't much longer before his alarm would go off to wake him up, but he was going to get every second he possibly could. Dean was leaving a little later in the morning, and then Kent would head to work for the rest of the day. Sylvia gathered some clothes and went into the bathroom to take a shower. She lingered under the hot water. If she was going to be missing out on sleep, at least she was going to enjoy her shower to its fullest.

After nearly an hour in the shower, Sylvia got out and took her time drying her hair and putting on her makeup so she was fully ready for the day. She went downstairs with a load of laundry and glanced out the window as she went by. The sun had just started to brighten up the horizon, and she could clearly see that the stretcher was still sitting exactly where it had been left before. That struck her as very strange, but she resisted the urge to go back outside.

She went downstairs through the finished part of the basement to the unfinished area where she loaded the washing machine and got it washing. As the drum was filling, she looked around, trying to think of any way this dull, sparse section of the house could be brightened up and made a bit more welcoming. She settled on asking Kent to paint the floor and seal it over with epoxy so it was something lighter than the dark-gray polished cement currently dominating the space.

With that settled and the load of laundry washing, she grabbed a basketful of towels she'd folded earlier but hadn't put away and brought them upstairs. She took another glance outside and noticed a police car now sitting in the driveway of Erin's house. The urge to go over tugged on her again. Ron did ask that they keep an eye on her. He would want to know what was going on, and maybe the police would have questions that Erin couldn't answer. But she still stopped herself and went into the kitchen to start a big breakfast.

The sun was coming up as she got some homemade biscuits in the oven. Then she decided to use more of her unexpectedly long morning by trying out a pastry recipe she'd been wanting to make but never felt like she had the time. The guys still weren't awake by the time she was finishing up, and she put the biscuits and pastries out on the dining room table. She was about to go back into the kitchen to make some eggs and bacon, but she caught sight of the window and noticed nothing about the scene out in front of the McCain house had changed. The ambulance was still there, lights flashing. The stretcher was still sitting in the street, untouched.

This was too much for her. She'd done her best to tamp down her curiosity and avoid going over to the house, but now she couldn't keep it away anymore. Something was very wrong. The sun was fully up. Hours had passed since she first noticed the lights, and they were still there. She needed to know what was happening.

She went down her driveway and across the street toward the house. As she was approaching, she realized that something was slightly different, but she couldn't put her finger on it. The lights flashing on the ambulance and the stretcher sitting out in the street without any siren or anyone around were eerie, and Sylvia felt a chill as she walked up to the front door. She rang the doorbell, but no one came to the door. She knocked, but there was still no response. The chill increasing, she cupped her eyes and looked through the glass to the side of the front door to see if she could see anything, but the inside of the house looked empty and still. She couldn't see or hear anyone. Not Erin. Not the EMTs.

"Sylvia?"

She looked up and saw Dean coming down the driveway. He paused to look both ways at the end of the driveway, then jogged across the street. She met him on the sidewalk.

"I came downstairs and noticed the food on the table but couldn't find you. I heard Kent in your room and thought you might be in there. I was bringing my stuff out to the car and saw you. What's going on?" he asked. "Why is the ambulance here?"

"I don't know," Sylvia said, shaking her head and wrapping her arms around herself. "I woke up a few hours ago because something startled me. I'm not sure what it was, but something woke me up. I saw the lights flashing, and when I looked outside, the ambulance was there. I saw an EMT get the stretcher out, but then they ran back inside, and it's all still here. I rang the doorbell and knocked on the door, but no one came to the door. I also didn't see anything when I looked in the windows. This is really freaking me out. I'm really worried about Erin."

"All right. Let me check it out," Dean said.

She was glad he was there. Standing there alone was making her feel even more uncomfortable, and she hoped he could use his skills as a private investigator to get to the bottom of what was happening. Everything would be fine, she told herself. There was an explanation. There had to be.

CHAPTER FIVE

THE WORRY IS OBVIOUS IN SYLVIA'S EYES. SHE'S LOOKING AT ME almost desperately, like she's depending on me to figure out why this ambulance is sitting here outside her neighbor's house. She said she looked inside from the windows and didn't see anything, which is definitely strange. There should have been emergency responders. Erin should be there. I walk up to the door and give a knock just for good measure. When no one answers, I walk around the side of the house to check the backyard. Sylvia hadn't mentioned checking behind the house, and I want to make sure something didn't happen outside.

I glance over the fence at the back of the house but don't see anything. This is very strange. I go back to the front of the house and return to the front door. I pound on it heavily with my fist.

"Erin? This is Dean Steele. I'm here with Sylvia from across the street. We just want to make sure that you're all right. Are you there?" I yell through the door.

THE WOMAN IN THE ATTIC

I give it a few seconds, waiting for any kind of reaction from anyone who might be inside, but nothing happens. I try the door handle and find it unlocked. I pause with it still closed, but the handle disengaged.

"I'm going to come inside now. The door is unlocked, so I'm going to come in and check on you." I want to announce my movements so I don't startle anyone, but I'm getting a heavy feeling that this isn't going to turn out well.

Opening the door, I look over my shoulder at Sylvia.

"Stay there," I tell her. "Do you have your phone with you?"

"Yes," she says.

"All right. If you hear anything, call 911."

She looks startled by the instruction, but it's safer to establish that now than for there to be any questions if I find myself needing help. I step inside the house and open the door wide, leaving it open as I venture into the entryway.

"Erin?" I call out again. "Anyone?"

I think I hear voices coming from further in the house, and I brace myself. I move deeper into the house, heading for the sound, and find myself in the kitchen. A small TV sits on the corner of the counter, and it's playing as if someone were watching while they were cooking. The room itself tells the same story. There are bowls of snacks set out on the counter and an empty bowl with a bag of popcorn sitting beside it. It looks like when whatever happened happened, Erin was preparing for a TV or movie binge.

I suddenly notice something on the floor. A few drops of dark-red liquid. There's more on the corner of the counter. This spurs me to look around the house with more determination. I clear all the rooms on the bottom floor and head upstairs. I look in the first bedroom and see nothing, then I open what I think is a door to the next bedroom. Instead, I see stairs leading up. They must lead to the attic. On a whim, I call up the steps to Erin, then check the doorknob. It's locked from the inside. I leave the door standing open and start climbing.

I'm not even at the top of the steps when I see something that makes my stomach drop. A mass of blond hair, then shoulders. There's a woman lying curled partway on her side on the attic floor, a pool of blood surrounding her bottom half and a fire poker sticking out of her leg. I know this isn't Erin. I met her just a few days ago, and this woman is taller and slimmer, with paler hair than Erin's dark bob. I don't want to touch her, even though it's my instinct to reach out to make sure that she's all right. She isn't moving. I know without checking her pulse that she's dead.

I run back down the stairs and out of the house. As I'm racing toward Sylvia, I notice a man coming across the yard toward her. She sees him and steps toward him.

"Bill," she says. "Thank goodness you're here. Dean, this is Erin and Ron's next-door neighbor Bill Meyer. He's a police officer."

I nod. "We need to call 911. Right now."

"What's going on? What happened?" Sylvia asks, sounding terrified. "Did you find Erin?"

"No," I tell her. "But I found someone. There's a woman's body in the attic."

"A woman's body?" Bill asks. "Is that why the ambulance is here? Where are the EMTs?"

"We don't know," I tell him.

"The ambulance has been here just like this for hours," Sylvia says. "I'm not really sure how long. I woke up a couple of hours before sunrise, and it was already sitting here. I saw EMTs near it, but they came inside, and it just hasn't left. I came over here to see if I could find out what was going on, but no one answered the door when I rang the bell or knocked, and I couldn't see anyone when I looked through the windows."

"I saw her over here and came to check and see if everything was all right. She told me what was happening, so I thought I'd take a look."

"Dean is a private investigator," Sylvia explains.

I nod. "The door was unlocked, so I announced myself and went inside. I heard voices, and it turned out to be the TV in the kitchen. There was food in the middle of being prepared, and I noticed blood, so I continued to search the house. I found the attic by accident but went into it, and that's when I found the woman. She is clearly dead."

Bill takes out his phone and calls emergency dispatch. He identifies himself and tells them that he needs backup and he believes there is a dead body so they will need the forensic unit. When he's finished, he looks at me again.

"I want to see what's going on in there," he says.

We go back into the house, and I show him around the exact way I went through the house, ending with showing him the woman in the attic and explaining the door was locked from the inside.

"This isn't Erin McCain," he says.

"I know," I tell him. "I met her a couple of days ago. I don't know who this is."

"Have you searched the rest of the house?" he asks.

"Just the downstairs. I didn't see the rest of this floor," I tell him.

THE WOMAN IN THE ATTIC

He takes out his gun and clears the rest of the floor, finding nothing in any of the rooms. As of this moment, Erin McCain and the two EMTs Sylvia saw are missing.

"I need to go back up to the body," he says. "I'm going to take a picture of her face and see if Sylvia might be able to identify her."

I stand at the bottom of the attic steps as he goes back upstairs, then we leave the house. Outside, Bill carefully shows the image to Sylvia. I can see that he took it in such a way that it doesn't show any of the blood. The way she's lying, her hair is partially obscuring her face, and it almost looks like she is sleeping, but I know it's much more horrific than that.

Sylvia steps back away from the picture on the phone and shakes her head, wrapping her arms around herself.

"No, I have no idea who that is."

"Sylvia?"

We look up and see Kent running from his house toward us.

"Dean? What happened? I was showering and getting ready. I didn't know you were over here. What's going on?"

We explain the situation to him, and Bill shows him the picture he took of the woman in the attic. He has the same reaction as Sylvia, shaking his head and saying he doesn't know who she is.

"Are you saying Erin is missing?" he asks.

"At least we don't know where she is right now," I clarify. "Everything is up in the air."

"What's with this ambulance?" Bill asks. "You said it's been here for hours?"

"Yes," Sylvia tells him. "It hasn't moved, and neither has the stretcher."

"This isn't from any of the local departments," Bill says. "I know there are a few private companies that have emergency and general medical transport, but I don't recognize any of these markings as being one of them."

"You don't?" Kent asks.

Bill shakes his head. "Give me a second. Let me call dispatch and find out how this got here."

He steps off to the side and calls dispatch, but he comes back to us with a puzzled expression on his face.

"I asked when they received the emergency call to come out here, and they said they didn't get any calls to come to this address until I just called them. Now, there wouldn't be an emergency call if someone called a private company directly. But why did they come out here, and where did they go?" he asks.

I walk up to the back of the ambulance and peer inside. Climbing up into it, I can immediately recognize how this vehicle differs from the conventional ambulances that would be dispatched from emergency services. While there are plenty of supplies and even some basic equipment, it lacks the more advanced equipment and features that would be necessary for a true life-saving vehicle. I notice a stack of blankets sitting on a shelf to the side and take one down. There's a marking in one of the corners, but it doesn't give any more information.

The screaming of the emergency responders arriving makes me put the blanket back and climb down out of the ambulance. Two police cars and a detective's vehicle pull up into the driveway and in front of the ambulance. The detective gets out of his car and comes over to us.

"Detective Mason Cartwright," he says, looking at each of us. He extends his hand to Bill. "Officer Meyer."

"Detective," he says. "Thanks for coming out."

"Why don't you tell me what's happening here? Dispatch said there's a body," the detective says.

"Yes. Up in the attic." He explains the entire situation. Even hearing it again doesn't make any of it make more sense. "I can confirm she is deceased. The only sign of injury is a fire poker in her leg."

"In her leg?" the detective asks, sounding as horrified as I feel.

The injury is gruesome, and I can't imagine dying from that kind of wound. Though if it hit her femoral artery, which is my assumption considering the amount of blood, death could have happened in a matter of only a couple of minutes. She might have lost consciousness within a minute. But the positioning of the body told me that she was trying to get to the steps, possibly without knowing that the door at the bottom was locked, anyway.

"Any identification yet?" Detective Cartwright asks.

"So far, no," Meyer answers. "I don't recognize her, and neither do Sylvia nor Kent. She doesn't live here."

"Why would she have been in the attic of a house she doesn't live in?" the detective asks.

It's a disturbing question all of us are wondering.

"The police car," Sylvia says. "That's what's different."

"Police car?" Detective Cartwright asks. "What do you mean?"

"When I looked out the first time, there was no police car here. But then, a while later, when I looked again, there was one. But then when I came over here, I thought something looked different and couldn't figure out what it was. That's what it was. The police car is gone," she says.

"Dispatch said there were no emergency calls made," Meyer tells her. "Are you sure that's what you saw?"

"I'm sure," she says.

"But Erin's car and the ambulance are still here," Meyer points out. "I somehow doubt everyone is piled into a squad car somewhere. So where are they?"

"Has anyone called Ron to find out if he's heard from Erin?" Kent asks.

The officers shake their heads.

"No. But that's a really good idea."

"I'll do it," he says.

He doesn't sound like he's looking forward to the task but that he understands it would be easier to get serious and concerning news like this from a friend than it would be from the detective. He steps away from the group, and I see him flip through his phone, then lift it to his ear. He comes back a few moments later without the relieved expression I was hoping to see on his face. That expression would have told me that Erin was somewhere safe and there was a simple explanation for this whole confusing situation. But he just looks more tense.

"Ron said he hasn't heard from Erin since last night. He tried to call her, but she didn't answer. He says he has no idea where she could be, and she always has her phone with her when she leaves the house, so he's really concerned. He's going to leave the conference and come back here. It will be several hours before he makes it back." Kent looks at me and gives me a firm pat on the back. "I'm glad you're here, Dean. Thank you."

"Dean Steele," Detective Cartwright says. "You've worked with that FBI agent. Griffin."

I nod. "Emma Griffin. She's my cousin. I've worked with her on some cases."

"I've heard of your reputation. If you can, I'd be happy to accept your help. Something like this is not exactly something our department is used to dealing with," he says.

"I'd be glad to help," I tell him. "I was planning on leaving today, but I can stay longer."

"I would appreciate anything you can do to help us," Cartwright says.

"Then I'm here."

CHAPTER SIX

"**O**FFICER MEYER AND I WERE TALKING ABOUT THE AMBUlance," I tell Detective Cartwright. "He pointed out that it doesn't belong to any of the local departments, and he doesn't recognize it as one of the private companies. Dispatch said that there weren't any emergency calls made to this address. If it was a private company, that would make sense, but it doesn't explain where the EMTs are. I went inside, and it didn't look like a true emergency vehicle. More like basic medical transport."

"Banes," he says, and a young officer who looks like he already feels in over his head comes over. "I want you to take official statements from Officer Meyer and Mr. and Mrs. Carruthers."

Officer Banes bobs his head and takes out a notepad and pen, poised to take down everything said to him. Leaving them to their statements, Detective Cartwright and I walk over to the ambulance and climb inside. I show him what I found and see the questions churning in his eyes.

"Did you search the front of the vehicle?" he asks.

THE WOMAN IN THE ATTIC

"No," I tell him.

He opens the driver's side door and gets in. I watch him look around, but there isn't anything up there for him to get any information from, so he gets back out. I get out too and meet him back in the yard. At this point, the other neighbors have started drifting out of their homes and gravitating over to the scene to find out what it's all about, compelling the other officers to guide them back and tell them to return to their homes. We're already going through enough at this point. We don't need spectators.

"We can find the vehicle identification number and search it to see who it's registered to," he says. "That will at least help us figure out who is missing. I'll get it towed to the police department so it can be processed."

As he makes the call to have the ambulance towed, the front door to the house opens again, and I look up to see two officers coming out carrying a body bag. They are removing the body of the woman from the attic. They carry her to a stretcher set up in the middle of the sidewalk and then wheel her to the waiting forensic unit vehicle. The FSU officer approaches Detective Cartwright, and the detective holds up a finger to ask him to wait. A few moments later, he finishes his call and tucks his phone away into his pocket.

"Yes?" Detective Cartwright asks. The officer's eyes shift over to me. "This is Dean Steele. He's a private investigator contracted by the police department for this investigation."

Though I haven't officially signed a contract with the department, I am looking forward to the formality. Rather than just being tacked on as an extra hand, I'm being officially recognized for my skills, which means I'll have greater access to the investigation and more leeway to handle elements of it on my own. It will eliminate the restrictions that often come along with not having a shield and official clearance, giving me more freedom, which I greatly appreciate.

"Frank Kingsley," the officer says to me. He turns his attention back to the detective after the cursory introduction. "I searched the body and found identification. Your victim's name is Sophie Berman. The address on the ID puts her living across town."

"Thank you," Detective Cartwright says.

"We'll transfer the body to the medical examiner's office," Kingsley says, giving a sharp nod before making his way to the vehicle to take Sophie Berman's body away.

Cartwright and I go back over to where Kent and Sylvia are finishing up giving their statements to Banes.

"Kent, Sylvia, do either of you know someone by the name of Sophie Berman?" Detective Cartwright asks.

They both look confused and shake their heads. Kent has his arm wrapped tightly around Sylvia like he's trying to keep her on her feet.

"Sylvia, have you ever heard Erin mention someone named Sophie?" I ask.

"No. We're just really getting to know each other," she says. "We haven't spent much time together."

"All right," Cartwright says.

"Can we go home now?" Kent says. "All of this has been really hard on my wife, and I'd like to get her some tea and let her try to relax."

"Of course," the detective says.

"Thank you."

"I'll be back later," I tell him.

He nods. "Let me know if you need anything else."

"I will."

They head back across the street, and I watch them until they make it to their sidewalk. Detective Cartwright is on the phone when I turn back to him. He's calling for more manpower to execute a search of the entire area of the house, including the woods behind the neighborhood. Right now we are juggling two disturbing realities: the strange death of Sophie Berman in the attic and the apparent disappearance of Erin McCain and the EMTs that were here for reasons no one knows.

The small police department of Briar Glen doesn't have the numbers of officers I would like for a search like this, but they turn out as many as they can for us to start combing the area for any sign of the EMTs and Erin McCain. We gather in front of the house, and Detective Cartwright assigns a handful of officers to create a perimeter, stopping any of the still-curious onlookers from getting closer to the house or interfering with anything that we're trying to do. They urge the neighbors to go back inside their homes and stay out of it, but I know even those who do comply with the instructions will likely find their way back outside. They might do it under the ruse of needing to do something else, like watering their lawns or checking the mail, or they might just walk out blatantly under the belief that they are on their own property so they can do whatever they want.

I know many others will be inside looking through the blinds just the way that Sylvia was early this morning.

We venture into the backyard and then into the wooded area behind all the houses on this side of the street. It's dense and undeveloped, with no walking trails or other features that would make this more like a park for the residents. I can see the children of the neighborhood using this as their own personal playground for adventures and exploration, much to the chagrin of their parents. But today it's quiet. If there are any children who play among these trees, their parents are keeping them inside as we scour the area.

It takes less than an hour for us to find Erin.

I'm walking carefully through the dense undergrowth with sweat beading on my forehead and stinging in my eyes when I hear one of the other members of the search party shouting out to the rest of us.

"Over here!"

It doesn't sound far from me, and I take off toward it as fast as I can move. Branches dig through my shirt, and undergrowth tangles at my feet as I run. I can see others gathering a few yards away, and as I get closer, I see something lying on the ground at their feet.

"Out of the way," Detective Cartwright calls from somewhere to my side, and I see him out of the corner of my eye going toward the group.

The officers part, and I see a woman on the ground. She's on her side with just her head turned up so her face is pointing upward toward the people surrounding her. As I get closer, I see that she's rocking back and forth slightly. Her clothing is ripped, and there's blood on her face and in her hair. As her rocking rolls her further forward, I see that the back of her shirt is tattered and there are cuts and scrapes on her skin.

"It looks like she was dragged," I point out to the detective.

"Where is he?" Erin mutters.

"Who?" I ask, crouching down so that I am closer to her.

"Where is he?" she asks again. "Is he all right?"

"Who are you talking about?" I ask.

"The EMT," she says. "The one who helped me. Where is he?"

I look up at Detective Cartwright. Erin continues to mutter, her words incomprehensible as her eyes flutter closed.

"No," one of the officers says, crouching down alongside us and reaching out to touch her face. "No, stay with us. Stay awake."

But there's no use. Erin goes unconscious, the muttering stopping and her head dropping forward.

"Get her out of here," Detective Cartwright demands. He picks up his phone and calls dispatch. "This is Detective Cartwright. I need an ambulance now."

"Should we move her, Detective?" one of the officers asks. "We don't know what kind of injuries she has."

"We can't leave her here in the woods," he says. "We need to get her out of here so that the ambulance can get to her. We're going to have to carry her."

To make sure she is as supported as possible, four men carefully scoop Erin into their arms and carry her out of the woods. They gently place her on the ground again once they get to her back patio, not wanting to bring her out in front of the neighbors still coming out to find out what is going on now that several hours have passed and the chaos is still unfolding on their usually quiet street.

It feels like it takes far too long for the ambulance to get here, but it's probably only a matter of minutes. Paramedics rush to load Erin onto the stretcher and put her in the back of the ambulance to bring her to the local hospital.

My brain is spinning with questions about what she was saying. Obviously, she encountered the EMTs that Sylvia saw, but where are they now? What happened to them? And what happened that brought them to the house in the first place? If they weren't called there, why did they respond? Is it possible that she's somehow contacted a private group rather than calling for an emergency response? If so, why? And how did she end up so deep in the woods?

"What the hell is going on here?" Detective Cartwright asks, seeming to reflect many of my own questions back to me just in the look in his gray eyes.

"She had to have been chased," I say. "It's the only reason I can think of that she would be in the woods like that. She must have been attacked, and then they dragged her through there but then gave up for some reason. Either it was just too difficult or they heard somebody else and thought they were going to get caught. Something happened that made them change their minds, and they left her. She was obviously seriously disoriented, but she could have gotten herself up and walked further, trying to escape, but because she was so disoriented, she went the wrong way. Adrenaline can do crazy things to a person. Even as injured as she was, she could have been able to go quite a distance."

"We need to get to the hospital," Cartwright says. "I want to find out everything I can about what she went through and be there if she's ready to talk. Any evidence that's on her needs to be collected as well."

"I'll call Kent," I tell him.

As we get into the car, I make the call.

"Do you have any updates?" he immediately asks me when he answers.

"I can't give you any details," I say. "But I need you to call Ron again and tell him to go straight to the hospital. That's all I can say right now. I promise I'll give you more when I'm able to."

"Can you at least tell me if you found Erin?" he asks.

I don't want to give out information that we haven't given her husband yet, but I know Kent can figure out that basic detail.

"Just tell him he needs to go to the hospital rather than his house," I say. "I'll talk to you again soon."

Them

They made a mistake.

This wasn't supposed to be this way.

As everything unfolded, there was nothing they could do. Nothing they could change. They were stuck.

She wasn't the one. It shouldn't have happened to her.

This could ruin everything.

But they weren't willing to let that happen. This was far too important for that.

They will just have to fix it.

CHAPTER SEVEN

We arrive at the hospital to see the ambulance already in the bay, the back doors open and the interior empty. Detective Cartwright and I rush inside and find out that Erin has been brought into the back, the emergency department, for initial treatment. Depending on the extent of her injuries, she may need to be transferred to the trauma unit.

As we are turning away from the nurses' station, Detective Cartwright's phone rings.

"Cartwright," he answers, turning his back to me and putting one hand on his hip as he starts to pace through the waiting area.

There are several other people in the waiting room, all of them watching us curiously. With the detective in his suit and me in a pair of jeans and a T-shirt, torn by the branches and with bits of the undergrowth clinging to me, we must be an interesting sight. But I think there's also an inherent curiosity that hovers around an emergency department waiting room. Everyone there has a story. There's a reason they are sitting in those chairs, listening to the low drone of whatever has been put on the TV that no one ever really is invested in. Some of those stories are so much more intense than others.

Looking around and wondering what the others in that room are going through makes you feel less alone. It takes some of the edge off the immediacy of the panic, the feelings of terror that can come with an emergency situation. And for those who are dealing with something simpler, something they know is going to have an easy outcome that just might require some medication and rest, it cuts through the boredom of waiting and the uneasy feeling that comes along with sitting in a hospital. Even when there isn't anything severely wrong, just being in this environment can be difficult to deal with.

I can feel the eyes on me as I walk over to the coffeemaker and fill two cups. These people are wondering about what happened to me, causing me to have bits of leaves stuck to my clothes, holes in my shirt, and sweat rolling down the sides of my neck despite the frigid air conditioner. They want to know who the detective is and why when he takes off his suit jacket to drape it across his arm as he talks, they can see how much he is also sweating and the remnants of the woods clinging to his shirt as well.

They want us to talk.

They want to be able to try to subtly point themselves toward us and listen to what we say to each other so they can try to decipher what we're going through. The emergency room is a place of whispers, and everyone there becomes an eavesdropper.

"Dean," the detective calls from the other side of the waiting area where I left him.

I grab the cups of coffee along with handfuls of cream and sugar and bring them toward him. He accepts one from me.

"Thanks."

"Cream and sugar?" I ask, offering the little cups and paper packets filling my fist.

"No, thanks. I take it black," he says. "I like to taste coffee in my coffee."

"You sound like my cousin Emma," I tell him.

I negotiate pouring cream and sugar into my cup while standing up, without anything in front of me to brace the cup on, and toss the trash into a nearby can.

"That call was from the department," he tells me. "It turns out getting in touch with Sophie Berman's next of kin is going to be easier than we might have thought."

"Why do you say that?" I ask.

"He's a nurse here at the hospital," the detective says. "He actually called dispatch earlier today, saying he hadn't heard from his sister the night before or this morning when he should have picked her up from work. Her car is apparently in the shop, and they had made plans for him to bring her here for her volunteer shift, but she wasn't there when he went to pick her up. An officer made the connection between that report and the body at the McCain house being identified as Sophie Berman. He is here at the hospital now, and there's a chaplain waiting to go with me to make the notification. Would you go with me so that we can also speak to him about the situation after making the notification?"

I understand Detective Cartwright's urgency in speaking with Sophie's brother, but I also am not looking forward to being there for a death notification. These conversations are one of the hardest parts of any career involving law enforcement or human interest. Even in my career as a private investigator, I have had to make several notifications of the deaths of loved ones to my clients, and it is always painful and emotionally charged.

I imagine anyone who has to face conversations like this probably feels the same way. It's never easy to have to meet with someone and let them know that a person they love is never going to come home. I don't know which is more difficult—making a notification to someone who already suspects that something terrible has happened but is still holding out all the hope they can possibly muster, or telling someone who is completely shocked by the situation. Both are brutal but have their own challenges. I hate shattering someone's hope and watching as everything they've built themselves up to endure dissolves away, leaving only their grief. But it's also excruciating to look into someone's completely unexpecting eyes and give them one of the worst news they will ever receive.

It sounds like Sophie's brother is in the former group. He has already contacted the police because he's worried about his sister, which means that a welfare check might have been performed where she lived. Obviously, they wouldn't have been able to go into her house without any other evidence that something was seriously wrong, and she couldn't have answered the door considering that we had found her body. But it would mean that her brother was told they couldn't get in touch with her either. He already knows something is wrong. Now it's just a matter of confirming it.

We meet the chaplain and explain to him what we are going to do. He nods calmly. He has a completely different role in the moments of someone finding out that their loved one is no longer alive. He isn't there to break the news or answer questions about what happened. He is solely a source of comfort and reassurance. In a way, I feel like he is coming with us as much for the detective and me as he is for Sophie's brother.

It takes a few minutes for us to track down Sophie's brother, Carson, and have him brought to a private room where we'll be able to talk to him without anyone else listening in on the conversation. He's already there when we walk into the room, and he immediately jumps to his feet, his eyes wild with worry.

"What's going on?" he asks. "Is this about my sister? Where is Sophie?"

"Mr. Berman, please have a seat," Detective Cartwright says, gesturing to the chair he just leaped out of. "I'm Detective Mason Cartwright. This is Dean Steele. He's a private investigator."

"Private investigator?" Carson asks, looking confused.

"We need to talk to you about a case that is developing right now," Mason says, pushing through the question so as not to let the conversation slow down. "Your sister is Sophie Berman, correct?"

"Yes," he says. "I called about her a few hours ago because I haven't heard anything from her. I messaged and called her last night, and she didn't answer. Then this morning when I went to her apartment to pick her up for her volunteer shift, she wasn't there."

"You said her car was in the shop," the detective says.

"Yeah," he says. "That's why I was bringing her here this morning."

"I'm very sorry to have to inform you that your sister was found dead this morning," Detective Cartwright says. "Right now, we don't have any specific details about her cause of death that we can share with you."

Carson recoils from the detective, pulling back away from him like he's trying to escape contact with the words he just said. He shakes his head frantically. The chaplain reaches over and rests a calming hand on his arm, murmuring to him as he tries to reconcile what he was just told.

"No… There has to be some kind of mistake," he says. "She has to be okay."

"I'm sorry," Mason says. "I know this is extremely difficult for you to hear, but we are going to need to ask you a few questions that might help us better understand what happened to her."

"Ask me questions?" Carson asks, sounding offended and angry. "You haven't even told me how my sister died or where you found her, and you want me to answer your questions?"

Any good rapport that might have existed between the two men is gone now. Carson sees Mason as the enemy and will resist anything from him now, even if it would be helpful in finding out what happened to Sophie. I look at the detective, silently asking him to step back for a minute and let me try. He catches on to the meaning in the look and physically steps aside so that I have clear access to Carson.

"Hi," I say. "I'm Dean. I'm so sorry for your loss. I don't know exactly what you're going through because I never had a sister, but I do know what it feels like to lose someone very important. Like the detective said, there aren't a lot of details that we can give you right now because this is all just unfolding as we speak. We don't know what happened, how, or why, which is why we need your help. I know it's really hard right now because you're just hearing this news, but it would be extremely helpful if you could talk to me just a bit about your sister. Can you do that?"

Carson nods. "How did she die?"

The image of the fire poker sticking out of Sophie's leg flashes in front of my face. I don't want to give him that image right now, so instead I give him a response that is truthful and generic without adding to the trauma of the conversation.

"We haven't gotten confirmation of the cause of death yet," I tell him. "As soon as we can, we'll let you know."

He nods again, seeming to accept this. "Where was she? Was she at home?"

"No. She was at the home of a couple named Ron and Erin McCain. Do either of those names sound familiar to you?" I ask.

"Yeah, Erin. She's a volunteer here at the hospital and a friend of my sister's. I don't know her. Sophie just talked to me about her some." His eyes suddenly snap up from the table. "Is she all right?"

"She's alive. She appears to have been attacked at her home and is currently being treated in the emergency room."

"Attacked?" he asks. "Someone attacked Erin? Does that mean someone attacked my sister? She was murdered?"

"Again, the cause of death has not been confirmed. Right now we don't know what exactly happened to her. She was found inside the home and did not appear to have the same signs of a physical attack as Erin. Her body has been transferred to the medical examiner, and we will get more information when her examination is complete," I say. "Did Sophie tell you anything about Erin going through problems?"

"No. Like I said, I don't know Erin. I think I might have talked to her once or twice, but it was just in passing. She seemed nice, but Sophie wouldn't tell me about anything personal going on in her life," Carson says.

"How about Sophie?" I ask. "Did she have anyone in her life that you can think of who might have wanted to hurt her? Did she have any enemies? An ex-boyfriend who might have been particularly disgruntled about their breakup? Anything you can think of?"

Carson shakes his head again, this time slower, as he seems to be thinking through everyone his sister knew, trying to come up with a viable answer to my question.

"No. She didn't tell me about anything like that. I can't think of any reason someone would be mad enough at her to want to hurt her. She didn't date very much, and the last time she went through a breakup, it was perfectly amicable. There wasn't any drama around it or anything.

"I'm not going to be like one of those people on the true crime shows who acts like every person who dies was the most wonderful, sweetest, friendliest, most welcoming person in the world who lit up every room they went into and made the world a better place just by breathing. I love my sister, but she was just a normal person. She volunteered here when she wasn't doing freelance graphic design work. She wasn't especially social, which is why I was glad when she told me about Erin. She just kind of lived life as it came, if that makes sense. I can't think of anyone who would want to hurt her or anything she might have gotten into that could have put her in danger," he says.

"And you said you tried to get in touch with her last night?" I ask.

"Yes," he says. "We talk pretty often, and I was calling her last night just to tell her that one of our favorite episodes of a TV show we used to watch together when we were younger was on and I was watching it. It wasn't anything really significant, but I thought it was strange that she didn't respond to my message or when I called her. But I figured maybe she was working or taking a shower. I didn't really know, but I didn't want to keep bothering her. Like I said, it wasn't anything significant. It wasn't like I needed something from her or I thought something was wrong. But then this morning when I went to get her, she didn't answer the door. I called, and I messaged. That's when I started to get worried."

"Do you have a key to your sister's apartment?" I ask.

"Yes," he says. "And I did go inside to check and make sure that she was all right. But she wasn't there."

"Would you bring me to the apartment and let me look around some?" I ask.

I know it's a bold request for this soon after notifying him of his sister's death, but there might be something there that could give us some answers.

Carson doesn't hesitate to nod, wiping tears away from his eyes and trying to straighten up like he's doing his best to control his emotions.

"That would be fine," he says. "I'll tell my supervisor that I need to leave."

"I'll go with you," I tell him. "I'm sure he will understand."

CHAPTER EIGHT

C ARSON'S EMOTION BREAKS THROUGH MORE AS WE TELL HIS supervisor the situation and he tells Carson to leave and take the next couple of days off if he needs to.

"I'll be back tomorrow," Carson vows. "I need to be here. I don't want to just sit at my house and think about this."

"If you change your mind, don't hesitate to take some time off," the supervisor tells him. "We will figure it out. And if you need anything at all, let me know."

"Thank you," Carson says, wiping away more tears.

We walk away from the supervisor and Carson looks at me.

"I'll get my stuff and meet you at the main entrance."

"We're parked at the emergency room, and I need to go get my car. Could you give me your sister's address and I will meet you there shortly?" I ask.

"Sure," he says.

He writes down an address on a slip of paper from the nurses' station and hands it to me.

"Thanks, I won't be long."

Detective Cartwright and I go back through the hospital to the emergency room entrance where he parked his car, and he drives me back to Kent and Sylvia's house. The ambulance that was sitting in front of the house for hours has been towed away, and most of the emergency vehicles are gone. All that's left is the crime scene investigation unit and a barrier of bright-yellow crime scene tape advertising to anyone who passes by that something very serious happened within the peaceful-looking white house.

I lift my eyes to the attic window at the top of the house. I wonder again what Sophie was doing in the attic of the house. Did she run away from someone?

"Let me know if you find anything at Sophie's apartment," Mason says when I climb out of the car. "I'm going to catch up with the CSU and see if they found any evidence around where we found Erin. Do you know when her husband is supposed to arrive back from his work conference?"

"It will probably be a little longer. He had a bit of a drive to get there, and I'm sure he needed to pack and everything before he left. I'll let you know if I hear anything," I say.

"All right, because we're going to need to talk to him as soon as he gets back," the detective says.

I nod and shut the door, jogging up the driveway to my waiting car. My keys are still inside where I tossed them early this morning when I noticed Sylvia across the street with the ambulance in front of the McCain house. I type the address Carson Berman gave me into the GPS on my phone, set it into the cradle attached to the windshield, and start to the apartment.

Like the forensic unit officer told us when they first identified Sophie's body, her apartment is across town, but Briar Glen is a small place, so the drive is only a few minutes. I think about the fact that Sophie's car is in the shop and wonder how she got to Erin's house. It's possible that Erin went and picked her up. They might have both worked a volunteer shift at the hospital yesterday evening and she simply brought her home with her afterward, but then why didn't she respond to her brother's message and call?

I make a mental note to contact the rideshare companies and find out if any of their drivers drove someone from Sophie's address to Erin's last night.

THE WOMAN IN THE ATTIC

A car I'm assuming belongs to Carson Berman is already in the guest spot designated for Sophie's apartment number, so I find an open unassigned spot and park. I grab my phone out of the holder and lock the doors before heading for the second-floor apartment. Carson is standing outside the door, leaning against the building as he stares out into the tree line behind the building.

"Carson?" I say.

He turns to look at me.

"Is it all right if I call you Carson?"

He nods. "Yeah."

I repeat the gesture back to him and look at the door to the apartment.

"I just couldn't bring myself to go in alone. I was just in here this morning, but I didn't know she was…" His voice drifts off, and I take a step slightly closer to try to give him some reassurance that he isn't alone.

"I really appreciate you doing this," I say. "We don't really know what's going on right now, and it's going to make a huge difference to have your cooperation as we're investigating. I know this isn't easy. It can't be. But you're doing what you can to help your sister, and that is really important."

"Thanks," he says.

He reaches into his pocket and pulls out his keys. He shows me one with a pink topper and gives a teary smile.

"When she gave me a copy of the key to her apartment, she thought it would be really funny to have the top pink so that I wouldn't forget which one it was. She said if anyone asked me why I had a pink key, I should just tell them it was for the Barbie Dream House," he tells me. "No one ever asked me, and I'm kind of disappointed I never got to use that line."

"It's a good one," I say. "Have the two of you always been close?"

"Ever since we were little," he says. "We were only a year apart, so we really grew up together. Our mother had to work a couple of jobs to keep us afloat, so we depended on each other most of the time."

He unlocks the door and opens it, stepping inside first. The door leads immediately into a small living room, and Carson walks over to a side table to flip on a lamp. I look around the neat space. The furniture is simple, matching brown suede with tables on either end of a couch, an oversized chair, and a coffee table in the middle. This furniture takes up the majority of the space, leaving only enough for a TV on the far wall.

I don't see anything that really gives me much of a feeling about who Sophie was as a person. There aren't any magazines on the coffee table or interesting art on the walls. It's just a neat, basic apartment for one person. To the opposite side of the living room is a dining area that has a puzzle set out on the table. I walk over to it and glance at the progress.

"Yeah, she really liked doing puzzles. She got a thrill out of piecing things together to make them just right," he says with a short burst of soft, mirthless laughter. "I used to tell her that spending her free time doing puzzles made her seem like an old woman, and drinking wine when she did it didn't make it any better. But there was just something about finding that perfect right piece and getting it into place."

She liked the control, I think to myself but don't say it. That's not a comment you make when someone has just gotten the news that their sister is dead.

It sounds judgmental and condemning, even though I don't mean it that way. It's just something that stands out. People who like to put together puzzles are often the same people who really like to have control and keep things in a very specific way in their lives. And since I know next to nothing else about this woman whose death I am now investigating, having that one little detail might end up meaning something to me.

"Maybe you could finish this one for her," I say, pointing out the image that sits nearly finished on the table.

"I should," he says.

"Would it be okay for me to look at the rest of the apartment?" I ask.

"Go ahead," he says.

We walk down a short hallway. The kitchen is right next to the dining room, and a washer and dryer take up a closet directly across the hall. Another closet is on the same side of the hall as the kitchen, and then the door to what I assume is her bedroom is at the very end.

I open the door and step into the faint smell of Sophie. It's one of those things that people don't think about in their own space but are easily recognizable when you go to someone else's home. Even when they aren't there, you can smell them. Their perfume. Their laundry detergent and fabric softener. Their shampoo. Even though I never met Sophie when she was alive, I know that the hint of smell in the bedroom has to be the unique scent of her, and it makes me feel a bit more connected to her.

The bed sitting with a large headboard against one wall is neatly made with a blanket folded at the foot and the pillows stacked at the head. A book sits on the nightstand, and I glance at the title. It's a beachy romance that looks like the spine has barely been cracked. She must have just gotten it, or she was very gentle with her books when she read them.

A dresser is up against the opposite wall, and I look at the few belongings organized on top. There's only one thing that doesn't appear to have been put in a specific place—a necklace with a unique silver pendant hanging from it. Looking at it for a few seconds makes me realize that it is designed to hold ashes.

"That was her favorite necklace," Carson tells me when he sees me pick up the necklace and look at it carefully. "She used to wear it all the time, but then the chain broke, and she almost lost it. That made her panic, so she never replaced the chain. She just keeps it here. It has our mother's ashes in it."

"I can understand why she would be so worried about that," I say. "I can't imagine losing something that precious."

I set the necklace down carefully on the dresser and take another look around the bedroom. This room has more personality than the living room. There are a couple of pictures on the wall of Sophie with Carson and with a group of people. There's a pair of shoes sitting beside the door to the en suite bathroom. It still has the same feeling of organization and control, but I feel like there's more of her here than in the living room.

"Does anything seem out of place here to you?" I ask.

Even though the apartment looks very neat and put together, he knows this place—and the woman who lived here—far better than I do. He might be able to recognize something as being off when it doesn't look that way to me.

"No," he says. "It looks pretty much like it always does. Sophie just isn't here."

I walk out of the bedroom and go into the kitchen. A coffee pot is filled with cold coffee on the counter. That isn't something I would ever expect in an apartment this well-kept.

"I noticed that when I came over this morning," Carson says. "She had her pot set to brew automatically so that it would be ready for her when she got out of the shower in the morning, then it would shut off. I came in here and checked to see if she had gotten her coffee. She did the same thing every single morning. She got up, took her shower and got dressed, had her first cup of coffee, did her makeup and hair, had a second cup of coffee, poured a third into her travel mug, then did whatever she was going to do that day. Volunteering at the hospital, running errands, just working, whatever it was she was going to do, she did all those things first.

When I came over this morning, I checked to see if she had coffee and saw that the pot had brewed, but she hadn't had any of it. That's what really pushed me to call the police. I knew that meant she wasn't here at all this morning." He shakes his head. "I don't know why I didn't clean out the pot. I just… I guess I just figured she would come back and want to clean it out in her specific way, so I didn't mess with it."

He walks over to the pot and takes it off the burner. He pours the cold coffee down the drain, filling the kitchen with its stale smell. He washes the pot, tearing up as he rinses it and sets it in the dish drainer. I have the feeling that somewhere in him, he's processing that he's going to have to go through this apartment and empty it out. If he is her next of kin, it means he is responsible for finishing everything for her, from getting rid of her possessions and emptying her apartment to making final arrangements for her and deciding how to memorialize her. It's not something I can fathom doing alone, and I hope that he has someone to support and help him through it.

"When was the last time you talked to Sophie?" I ask.

"Yesterday afternoon," he tells me. "She called me to tell me that her car still wasn't ready, even though they thought it was going to be. She said they were still waiting for a part and it might be a few more days. She was really frustrated. That's when we made the plan that I would pick her up this morning."

"How has she been getting around without her car?" I ask.

"I'm not sure. Rideshares, I guess. She might have asked her neighbor or someone for a ride if she needed to go somewhere," he says. "But it had only been a couple of days, and I know that one of the other volunteers from the hospital gave her a ride for her volunteer shift because I had to be there a lot later than her."

"Erin McCain?" I ask.

"No," he says, shaking his head. "A guy named Trevor. He lives somewhere close around here, apparently."

"You don't know him?" I ask.

"No. She just told me about him when she said she got a ride."

"All right. Well, thank you for letting me do this. I really appreciate it. I'll let you know if I have any other questions, and I'll update you when I have more to tell you," I say.

I leave the apartment wishing there had been more there, anything that might have given me some clue about Sophie so I can begin to understand what happened to her. But she didn't die at home. Her death is directly related to Erin McCain, and I need to find out why.

CHAPTER NINE

My stomach is rumbling as I leave the apartment, and I realize I haven't eaten anything today. The breakfast Sylvia made early this morning, a time that now feels like days ago, went untouched as I responded to the situation unfolding at the McCain house and never went back. I drive through a fast-food restaurant to grab something quick and eat it on the way back to the hospital. I haven't gotten any updates from Mason, and I want to check in with the doctors about Erin.

Not knowing if they have moved her to another floor yet, I park in the emergency room lot again and go inside. The nurse behind the desk recognizes me as I come through and beckons for me to come over to her.

"Erin McCain has been moved upstairs. Fourth floor," she tells me.

"Thank you," I tell her.

I head back through the sliding glass doors so I can move my car around to the main entrance. As I am walking up to the door, I see someone running toward it and immediately recognize him.

"Ron!" I shout.

He pauses and looks around like he's heard me but can't see me. I wave and jog toward him. He looks disheveled and on the brink of panic.

"Dean," he says, "Kent called me and told me to come to the hospital rather than go home. I got here as fast as I could. What's going on? Did you find Erin? Is she all right?"

I rest a hand on his shoulder to try to calm him.

"Come on over here," I tell him, leading him away from the middle of the parking lot where we'd stopped.

I bring him over to the sidewalk to the side of the main entrance to the hospital, pausing with him under the portico and giving him a few seconds to catch his breath. But he doesn't seem capable of calming down. His breath is ragged in his chest, and his eyes flash frantically back and forth as he shifts his weight from foot to foot like he can't be still.

"Where is Erin? I need to know what happened to my wife," he demands.

"Ron, I need you to take a deep breath. This is a lot. I know it is. But you need to calm down and listen to me," I say.

He puts his hands on his hips and does what I say, drawing in a long breath. He hesitates for a second, then lets it out slowly. I nod encouragingly, and he takes another. The tension in his shoulders seems to lessen slightly, but he's still rocking back and forth.

"We found Erin in the woods behind the house. She was really deep in them and looks like she went through a violent attack. She was awake when we found her, but she lost consciousness before we transferred her to the hospital. As of right now, I haven't gotten any further information about her. From what I saw, her injuries are pretty serious, but I can't tell you any more than that."

"I need to know what happened to my wife," he says again, louder and more intensely this time, as if he would be able to force the knowledge out of me if he was just insistent enough.

"Ron, I'm sorry, but I don't know exactly what happened to her. That is everything I can tell you about her condition right now. I can bring you inside and see if the doctors will let you see her," I offer.

"Yes," he says.

"All right. They just told me that she's been brought to the fourth floor. Let's go," I say.

THE WOMAN IN THE ATTIC

We go into the hospital and use the elevator to get up to the fourth floor. I walk up to the desk.

"Erin McCain please," I say. "This is her husband, Ron."

I gesture to Ron, who has already started to pace the waiting area behind me. He's full of too much pent-up energy and nervousness.

"Give me just a second," the nurse behind the desk says and picks up the phone beside her.

I walk up to Ron and put a hand on his back.

"We're going to find out what happened," I reassure him. "Whatever Erin went through, they are taking good care of her, and we're going to find out who did it. I've been asked to be a part of the official investigation, so you know I'm right here and will keep you as updated as I possibly can."

Even as I'm saying it, there's something bothering me. It's just prickling at the back of my mind, and I'm trying not to focus on it, but it's hard to keep it quiet. I ignore the questions and focus on trying to calm the frantic man down. He stops pacing and looks at me with a blend of emotions in his eyes that's difficult to discern.

"The doctor will be right out," the nurse tells us.

"Thank you," I say.

A few moments later, a doctor comes from down the hallway and makes eye contact with me first, then Ron, like he's trying to figure out who each of us is in the context of the case.

"Dean Steele," I tell him, extending my hand. "I'm a private investigator helping with the case. This is Ron McCain, Erin's husband."

"Dr. Bishop," he says, shaking each of our hands. "Mr. McCain, if you'd like to come with me, I can fill you in on what's going on with your wife."

The doctor takes a step down the hall and gestures for Ron to follow him, but he hesitates. Ron looks at me.

"I don't want to go alone," he says. "Dean can come with me."

"You know I will use any information I get as part of my investigation," I say, just wanting him to understand that offering for me to go with him was more than just wanting to have emotional support while he finds out the extent of the injuries done to his wife.

"I know," he says. "I want you to find whoever did this."

"That's fine," Dr. Bishop says.

We follow him down the hallway to a room similar to the one where we gave Carson notice of his sister's death and sit down.

"First, I want you to know that we do have your wife sedated at the moment. I wanted to put her under so her body will experience less stress and have a better opportunity to heal," the doctor says.

"How long are you going to have her like that?" Ron asks.

"I can't tell you for sure right now. We're going to keep her under close observation and bring her out of the sedation when we think it's the best time. I'll keep you updated," he says. "As for her condition, I'm sure the police have told you that she was attacked and suffered some extensive injuries. She has suffered a head injury, and there are various cuts and punctures on her body. There are also indications that she was dragged across the ground for some distance. We've removed splinters and other debris from the wounds and are now working to prevent infection."

"Who would have done something like this to her?" Ron asks.

"That's something we're hoping you're going to be able to help us figure out," I tell him.

"There aren't any indications on the body that tell us who is responsible," the doctor says. "We searched for DNA but didn't find anything under her fingernails and no sign of sexual assault. That doesn't mean that she didn't fight back, but it's entirely possible whoever did this was wearing long sleeves, gloves, and other coverings that prevented Mrs. McCain from getting any biological material under her nails. Until we're able to talk to her about it, we won't know for sure."

"Is she going to remember what happened?" Ron asks. "Something this awful... Is she going to have the memory of it?"

The question makes the hair stand up on the back of my neck, but I don't show the reaction.

"I don't know," the doctor says. "Some people retain everything that happened even after something this apparently traumatic. Others won't have any memory at all. Others are able to remember some things but can't bring back everything. Again, we won't know until we're able to talk to Mrs. McCain directly."

I notice the doctor is speaking vaguely, not giving full explanations of what they found when they examined Erin. It's like he's trying to protect Ron from the realities of what his wife went through, even though he knows he's going to have to find out, eventually.

"Can I see her?" Ron asks.

Dr. Bishop looks uneasy at the request, like he doesn't really want to let Ron back to see Erin, but he doesn't have cause to outright deny him. He stands.

"I'll bring you to her room," he says. "But remember, she is not in good condition, and she is not conscious. You might find what you see very disturbing."

The warning doesn't put Ron off. He simply nods and stands up alongside the doctor.

"I want to see her," he says.

The doctor leads us further along the hallway to a closed door. He eyes me and looks at Ron as if he's silently asking whether he wants me to go in with him or if he would rather the doctor request I stay outside. I have already seen Erin. I know what she looked like before the medical staff was able to get to her. It's not going to be a shock to me to see her now, though Ron might want privacy as he copes with what she's going through. But he did say he didn't want to go through this alone, so if he decides that he wants me to go into the room with him, I'm going to go.

"You can't stay with her for very long right now," Dr. Bishop says. "We still have some work to do with her and will be back shortly."

The cool way he says that they have work to do on her seems to be intended to be less difficult to hear, but it ends up sounding more ominous than if he had just given specifics. He opens the door and steps in first, moving aside to let Ron in. He doesn't say he doesn't want me in there with him, so I follow right behind.

As soon as the doctor pushes aside a curtain that was pulled around the bed and Ron steps up beside it, his hand flies up to cover his mouth. I stand at his side and look down at Erin. She has a bandage on her head and on various injuries across her body. Her face is discolored and swollen, looking even worse than it did when we first found her. She has an IV in her arm and machines attached to her body to monitor her condition as the sedation keeps her unconscious to give her body a chance to recover.

"Can I touch her?" Ron asks.

"Be gentle," the doctor says. "Don't move her around very much."

Ron picks up one of Erin's hands and kisses her knuckles, then presses the hand to the center of his chest.

"I'm here," he says. "I'm right here, honey."

I know she can't hear him, but it's reassuring to him to talk to her, so we stand quietly while he continues to reassure her that he's here and will be when she wakes up. I pay attention to what he's saying and the way that he's acting as he tries to comfort her. We haven't given him all the information yet about what happened, and I know I'm going to need to make sure he knows everything as soon as possible. I rest a hand against the center of his back and lean in slightly so I can speak to him in a lowered tone.

"I'm going to step right outside and make a quick phone call," I say. "I'll be right outside."

Ron sniffles and takes Erin's hand in both of his, not looking at me as he bobs his head. "Okay."

I look at the doctor and point toward the door. "I'm just going to be outside."

I step out of the room and pull the door closed behind me so that they can't hear my conversation inside the room. Stepping to the far side of the hallway, I call Detective Cartwright.

"Hey," I say when he answers. "This is Dean. I am up at the hospital, and Ron McCain is here. He is in with Erin right now. He hasn't been notified of Sophie's death in the house yet, has he?"

I am sure he hasn't, but I ask just for confirmation and also as a gentle prodding to the detective to remind him that this important step needs to be done. We don't want Ron to hear about the dead body being found in his attic from someone else—or worse from the media, which is going to get the story whether we want them to or not.

"No. No one has had a chance to talk to him. If you're there with him, will you tell him?" he asks. "See if maybe he can tell you something about her being at the house or about her friendship with Erin."

"Sure thing," I say. "I'll give you a call after we talk."

"Thanks, Dean," he says.

I end the call and am just putting my phone back in my pocket when the door opens and Ron steps out into the hallway. His eyes are red, and he looks like he's fighting to keep more emotion from coming out. It's the kind of reaction I would expect from a man who has just found out that his wife was brutally attacked but who wants to maintain a sense of strength and stability. Which is why I'm noticing it.

"They need to work on her some more," he tells me. "They said I can come back and see her again later."

"Want to go get some coffee?" I ask. "There are a couple of things we need to talk about."

CHAPTER TEN

"I DON'T WANT TO LEAVE THE HOSPITAL," RON SAYS. "JUST IN case they tell me I could go back and sit with her. They said they would call me when they are done with what they need to do right now so I can go back in with her."

"That's fine," I tell him. "We can just go down to the cafeteria and get some coffee, then maybe go sit out in one of the courtyards. It's a nice day, and we can talk away from everybody else."

Ron gives me a questioning look. "Talk away from everybody else? What's going on?"

"There are a few more details about what went on that I need to talk to you about," I tell him. "But I think it's important that we talk somewhere as private as possible."

We go down to the cafeteria and get coffee and a couple of pastries, then bring them out to a small meditation garden set in the center of the hospital. It's beautiful, with trees creating pools of shade over benches and a water feature at the end, giving off a cool mist and creating a soothing sound. I can see people finding a tremendous amount of comfort in a place like this when they are going through the difficulty and trauma of a loved one being in the hospital.

Ron and I sit down on one of the benches, and I take a sip of my coffee. I got it iced in favor of the warm summer weather and take a second to savor the refreshing cold.

"What is it that you wanted to talk to me about?" Ron asks impatiently.

"Do you know anyone by the name of Sophie Berman?" I ask.

He looks like he's thinking for a few seconds. "Sophie Berman… That sounds really familiar. Oh yeah, that's a friend of Erin's from work. They're both volunteers at the hospital. Why?"

"Sophie was found dead in the house before we found Erin," I tell him.

There might have been a gentler way to approach it, but I think that being straightforward and right to the point is much better for this conversation. I need information as quickly as I can get it, and beating around the bush or sugarcoating the situation isn't going to get that done for me.

Ron's mouth falls open, and a few sounds come out like he's trying to say something but can't exactly get the words together. His hand starts to shake, and I take the coffee cup from it so he doesn't drop it.

"Dead?" he asks. "What do you mean Sophie was found dead in my house?"

"I don't know exactly what Kent told you when he called you, but very early this morning, Sylvia saw an ambulance outside of your house, and it was out there for quite some time. She went over to see what was going on and couldn't find anybody. She wasn't able to find Erin or the EMTs that should have been with the ambulance. She was extremely concerned, and when I went over there to check and see what was going on, I offered to check inside the house to see if I could find anything.

"The front door was unlocked, and so I went inside. The kitchen looked like she had been preparing some snacks while watching a TV show, and I saw a small amount of blood on the counter and on the floor, which made me check the rest of the house. I thought that the door to the attic was the door to a bedroom, but I went up into the attic when I saw that the light was on and found Sophie's body. At this time, her cause of death has not been confirmed, but there was a serious injury to her leg. We don't know what happened right now," I tell him.

"Somebody killed Sophie in my house and attacked my wife?" he asks. "I don't understand what's happening."

"Neither do we," I admit. "But I've been asked to be an official part of this investigation, like I told you. So we're trying to help each other right now. I mentioned the kitchen looked like she was making some snacks. But this all happened in the extremely early hours of the morning. Is that something that sounds like a normal behavior for Erin?"

Ron stares at the pastry still in his hand for a few seconds, then looks up at me with an almost startled expression, like he's forgotten that I'm sitting here.

"Yeah," he says. "Sometimes she has a lot of trouble sleeping. Especially when I'm out of town. If she can't get to sleep, she has this habit of getting a bunch of snacks and sitting up watching infomercials and reruns of old TV shows until she falls asleep."

"Did you talk to your wife last night?" I ask.

"I talked to her before going to dinner with some associates. She didn't mention anything about Sophie coming over, but that doesn't really mean anything. It could have been a last-minute plan. But I don't understand why Sophie would be over at the house so late."

He puts the pastry down and leans forward to rest his elbows on his knees, putting his face in his hands.

"I can't believe this is happening. I should have been there. I feel so horrible that I didn't know what was happening. I wasn't there for her. I didn't know what was happening to her."

"You couldn't have known," I tell him, trying to reassure him even as his words again strike me as odd. There's something about this whole situation that isn't right. "You said you were going to have dinner with some associates. So the business trip was still going as planned?"

"Yes," he says. "It isn't uncommon for me to have dinner with different people during the conference so I can continue networking. A lot of these people, I don't see in person any other time except for these conventions and other events, so we try to find ways to spend more time together."

It sounds like more explanation than was really necessary, like he's trying too hard to get me to believe what he's saying. I have a gut feeling I already know why.

"And it was all right for you to leave the convention early?" I ask.

"Of course," he says. "This is an emergency, and my wife is the most important thing to me. Her safety and well-being are my priority. Everybody at the conference understood why I needed to leave."

"That's good," I say. "If you could give me just a second, I need to make another phone call really fast. I'm sorry."

"It's fine," he says. "Go ahead."

I stand up and set his coffee on the bench beside him so he can drink it if he wants to. He's still staring down at the ground as I walk away and call Detective Cartwright again.

"I just told Ron McCain about Sophie Berman's death," I tell him.

"How did he take it?" he asks. "Did he know her?"

"I don't think he did," I say. "He said that she was a friend of Erin's, just like Carson told us. But it didn't sound to me like he had ever even met her. He was really surprised to hear that she was at the house so late. He did explain that it wasn't uncommon for Erin to stay up late at night and watch TV, so that makes the kitchen make more sense. But I think there's something else going on."

"What do you mean?" he asks.

"Ron seems legitimately upset, but he has said a couple of things that have struck me as kind of suspicious. And I noticed that it didn't take him as long as it should have to get back from the conference. Even really rushing because he was upset and worried about his wife doesn't account for it. It should have taken him another hour or two at least," I say.

"What do you think it means?" he asks.

"I don't think Ron McCain was at that conference last night," I tell Detective Cartwright. "I think something else is going on, and we need to make sure."

"Let me make a couple of phone calls," the detective says. "I will give you a callback when I get an answer."

"Sounds great, thanks," I say.

I go back to Ron, who is now sipping his coffee and staring at the waterfall.

"Everything all right?" he asks. "Did you find out something else?"

"I might have," I tell him. "Can you explain to me how you got back here so fast?"

He looks over at me with a quizzical expression on his face. I notice his hand tighten around his coffee cup.

"What do you mean?" he asks.

"If you were at the conference when Kent called you, how did you get back here so fast? You would have had to pack everything up from your hotel room and then make the several-hour drive back. It should have taken you quite a bit longer than it did to get here," I say.

"I was worried about my wife," he says defensively. "I just got a phone call that she was missing and then later got one that I needed to come to the hospital rather than coming home. I wasn't exactly keeping to the speed limit or following all the traffic laws on my way back here. All that mattered to me was getting here as fast as I possibly could."

"And I can understand that," I say. "But even with all of that, you got here a lot faster than I think would be possible."

"What are you suggesting?" he asks.

"I'm not suggesting anything. I'm giving you the opportunity to tell me the truth so that we know what's actually going on here. Remember, I am investigating not just the attack on your wife but also a suspicious death inside your house. I need to know what was really happening with everyone in their immediate circle, and that focus is directly on you right now," I say.

"I can't believe you're questioning this," Ron says, standing up and glaring down at me. "I'm trying to deal with all of this being thrown at me, and all you can do is hint around that I'm lying about something because I didn't take as long to get here as you think I should have."

I stay calm even though he's escalating, wanting to keep the conversation civil and stop him from causing a scene, which is where it looks like he's heading. He starts to stalk back toward the doors to the hospital, and I stand up.

"Detective Mason Cartwright, the detective heading up this case, is currently making calls to check up about the conference and your attendance in it," I say. "We're going to know soon enough, so you might as well come forward and be honest about this, Ron. I'm just trying to find out what happened."

Ron stops, his head falling back as he lets out a heavy sigh. He keeps his back to me for a few seconds, takes a sip of his coffee, then turns around to face me.

"Fine," he says. "Fine." He comes back toward me. "I wasn't at the conference last night."

"All right. Why don't we sit back down, and you can explain it to me," I say.

He looks at the bench reluctantly, like he's not sure about sitting down, but then complies.

"The conference wasn't as long as I said it was going to be," he tells me. "I also skipped the last day so I could come back earlier."

"And why is that?" I ask. I have a feeling I already know the answer, but I need to hear it from him.

He sighs again. His expression is defeated with tinges of fear around the edges of his eyes.

"I came back to see my girlfriend," he says.

The words all come out in a burst of air, and he hangs his head, shaking it back and forth before running his fingers through his hair and covering his mouth with his hands. It's like he can't stop moving, can't choose a gesture or position that feels right in this tense moment.

"You have a mistress," I say.

"Yes, if you want to put it that way," he says. "But that doesn't mean that I don't love my wife. It doesn't mean that I tried to do anything to her. I just need…" He lets out a dry, humorless chuckle. "I can't even believe I'm having this conversation right now. I've done everything I can to stop Erin from ever finding out about Melissa. Because I don't want my marriage to end. I don't want anything to happen between the two of us. Melissa understands that. She knows that I just need some more excitement in my life. Erin and I are good together. We love each other. But I need more."

"So you've been cheating on her," I say.

"You can judge me if you want to," he says. "But it doesn't mean I did any of this."

"I'm not judging you," I tell him. "I'm just trying to understand exactly what happened."

"Exactly what happened is that I told Erin and everyone else that the conference was going to be longer than it really was. I skipped a half day of social activities so that I could drive home to see Melissa. We were traveling for a spontaneous getaway when Kent called. That's how I was able to get back as quickly as I was," he says.

"Where does Melissa live?" I ask.

"She lives in Briar Glen," he tells me.

"So you were in town the night that your wife was attacked and Sophie Berman died?" I ask.

"Yes, but I had absolutely nothing to do with either one of them. I am having an affair, yes. I will admit that. And my wife didn't know about it. I didn't want her to know about it. I know it would absolutely break her heart to find out. But I would never do anything to hurt her. Like I just said, I don't want my marriage to end. I don't want anything to change," he says.

"You just want some more excitement," I say.

His eyes narrow. "I didn't hurt my wife."

"Ron, you know there's no way that this can be kept a secret," I say. "Erin is going to find out. We're going to have to use this information as part of the investigation. I will make sure that you are the one to tell her if that's what you want, but I can't promise that the offer will stay on the table for long. We're going to be investigating your whereabouts and your movements, and we're going to need to question Erin about her knowledge of the affair and any suspicions she might have had, as well as talk to her about the state of your marriage. You understand that."

"I understand. I'll tell her as soon as I can," he says. He takes another deep sip of his coffee and stares at the cup for a few seconds. "I guess everything is going to change now."

"I think that's a pretty good bet," I say. "But you have to let Erin be the one to make that decision. I can't speak for her."

"I should have gone to couple's counseling with her," he says.

The inane comment almost makes me angry. We're sitting outside the hospital while his wife fights for her life and the police try to find out why there was a dead woman in this man's attic, and he is just now lamenting that he should have gone to therapy rather than turning to another woman. I want to be as neutral as I can, but he's making this very difficult.

"I'll need Melissa's full name and her contact information," I tell him. "So that we can get in touch with her and get her side of the story. I'll have to ask you not to contact her at all until we've spoken with her."

"That's fine," he says.

He gives me the phone number and address for Melissa Garrison, finishing just as his phone rings. He picks it up, and his eyes squeeze closed tightly.

"Thank you." He hangs up. "That was the nurse. I can go back and sit with Erin now."

CHAPTER ELEVEN

Putting the small notepad I wrote the information down on back in my pocket, I stand up and extend a hand toward Ron. We're going to be interacting much more throughout this investigation, and I want to keep things as friendly and not volatile between us as possible.

"I'll be in touch," I say.

Ron doesn't take my hand. "The doctor asked that you come up with me," he says.

"Oh," I say, unsure what to think of the request. "All right."

We return to the fourth floor in chilly silence. I hope that the doctor isn't asking me to come up to be emotional support for Ron because then I have more bad news for him. I want Erin to pull through and recover fully from everything she suffered. I know she has a long way to go, but I don't want to hear that it is even worse than expected.

Dr. Bishop is waiting for us when we get off the elevator. He gives a slight nod toward Ron.

"You can go in. We're done with Mrs. McCain for right now. You should be able to stay with her as much as you want to for the next few hours," he says.

"Thank you," Ron says. He looks at me as he takes a tentative step down the hallway.

Dr. Bishop gestures toward the room.

"I just need to speak with Mr. Steele for a moment," he says. "It won't take long."

Ron hesitates, but then he turns and makes his way down the hallway toward his wife's room. The doctor looks at me.

"What did you want to speak with me about?" I ask.

"If we can go into the private room, that would be better," he says. "I want to protect Mrs. McCain's privacy as much as I can."

We go back into the small room where we first spoke with Ron, and he closes the door behind us.

"I wanted to have a word with you about Mrs. McCain when she first came into my care. I know that she went unconscious when she was first found in the woods, but she did regain consciousness in the emergency room. She was still conscious when she was transferred up to my unit, and she had begun talking. The doctors and nurses in the emergency room had been trying to get her to talk about what happened to her and communicate anything about what she was feeling, but they weren't able to get anything out of her," he says.

"What was she talking about when you heard her?" I ask.

"It was fairly incoherent. She was essentially just rambling, and a lot of what was coming out of her mouth was just sounds or partial words that we couldn't really understand. The only things I was able to get from her were about an EMT. She was continuously asking for the EMT who helped her. She asked where he was and if he was all right. It didn't really make sense to me, but I thought it might have something to do with the investigation, so I wanted to bring it to your attention," he says.

"Thank you," I say. "She was actually talking about that when we first found her, as well. It's something we're trying to figure out. As of right now, the EMTs who were there have not been found or come forward. There is still a search being conducted in the area where she was found, but nothing has been found as of the last update I received. So much of the information we need is going to come from Erin herself, but getting that from her isn't possible right now."

"It isn't," Dr. Bishop says. "But she's responding well to treatment, and hopefully, we will be able to pull her out of sedation relatively soon. Whether she is up to talking to you about what happened is going to be something we have to find out then. I will keep you updated on her condition and let you know as soon as we're able to wake her up and she's willing to talk."

"I really appreciate your cooperation," I say.

Leaving the small room where I was talking to the doctor, I go to Erin's room. Ron has pulled a chair up to the side of the bed and is sitting, holding her hand again. He gazes into her face. And I can't stop thinking about his confession about Melissa Garrison. The way he's looking at Erin seems like a genuinely concerned spouse, but I can't ever let myself use pure emotion as evidence in an investigation. He is very aware that he is being watched and evaluated. The way he's behaving right now could be genuine, but it could also be a carefully constructed ruse begun before we knew he was lying about the conference and where he was when he got the call from Kent.

"I just want to let you know that I'm going to be in the hospital for a little while longer, and if you need me, you can call me," I tell Ron, giving him my business card. "I'm also still at Kent and Sylvia's house for now, so you can find me there if you need something."

"Thank you," Ron says, looking back at Erin. "Dean," he says, stopping me when I'm nearly back to the door.

"Yes?"

"I love my wife," he says. "She doesn't know about the affair because I never wanted her to get hurt."

"That isn't any of my business beyond it being a part of the investigation," I tell him.

"No, but I want you to hear it," he says. "If I wanted to be married to someone else, I would have just left Erin and found someone who wants to get married. That's not what I was after, and it's not what Melissa wants. She is on the same page as I am. We see each other when we can. We enjoy our time together. That's it. I don't love her. She doesn't love me. There have been no promises about my marriage ending so that we can be together, and she knows that if she meets someone else who she would rather be with, then there's nothing holding her back.

Erin and I went through a very difficult patch about a year, year and a half ago. I thought our marriage was going to be over then, and I was devastated. Even when we were fighting all the time and it didn't seem like we could get along for a single day, I still loved her with my entire being and didn't want to be without her. The thought of losing her was so painful, and I did everything I could to rebuild what we had. Things were really good after that for a while, but then I started feeling stagnant.

It was just the same day over and over again, and there wasn't anything interesting or new in our lives anymore."

He looks at Erin again, and I cringe at the thought of her possibly being able to hear any of this. I hope she can't. This doesn't feel like the time or the place to be having this conversation, but I can't stop him.

"I didn't want to ever feel again the way I did when we were having such a hard time. That was the worst feeling I've ever had, and I didn't want to face that kind of pain again. I especially didn't want to even think for a second about ending our marriage. But I knew I needed something to make life more interesting. To give me a little bit of a spark. When I met Melissa on a work trip and found out that she worked for a different company but lived in Briar Glen, it just seemed like the universe was giving me a sign."

"You think the universe gave you a sign to cheat on your wife?" I ask.

"I'm not asking you to agree with what I did," he says. "It's very obvious the way you feel about me and the decisions I've made. But I am asking you to open your mind a little and understand why I've done this. I never intended for Erin to find out. In fact, I felt like my time with Melissa was actually improving our marriage. I was happier and felt more adventurous and energetic, which rubbed off on Erin. We were doing even better, and that was great.

"From the very beginning, I made sure that Melissa understood there was nothing romantic about us. We were not going to fall in love. This was not about us being together as a couple someday. She agreed completely. She isn't interested in any kind of commitment that goes beyond dinner reservations or a weekend away. I think that's going to change for her someday. She'll meet someone who totally sweeps her off her feet and realize that there is something beautiful and wonderful about committing yourself to one person. But maybe she won't. And either way, she's happy with her own decisions and what she wants in her life. This was never supposed to be something that Erin found out about because it never had anything to do with her."

"Let me ask you something," I say. "Did you ever talk to Erin about being bored or thinking that there wasn't enough excitement in your life?"

Ron shakes his head. "No."

"Then how can you possibly say it wasn't about her?" I ask. "You didn't even give her the chance. You're right. I don't agree with what you did. And I don't even think that I fully understand it. I can't wrap my head around someone saying they are so in love with their spouse and have a good marriage if they are giving their time, energy, and happiness over to someone else. You might not think that you were doing anything wrong because Erin didn't know and couldn't be hurt, but I promise you, all that time you took from her and gave to Melissa was felt."

I walk out of the room before he can continue the conversation. This isn't something I want to talk about anymore. I'm still suspicious of him no matter how much he gushes about his love for Erin and wants me to believe that his marriage is something unconventional but functional and happy.

I go back downstairs to the meditation garden and call Detective Cartwright again. I tell him what the doctor told me about Erin regaining consciousness and babbling about the EMT.

"The search team searched the entire woods behind the neighborhood and didn't find anything," he tells me. "No sign of any other people anywhere near her house. There's a BOLO out, but it's really hard to let people know what they're looking for when there's no description other than 'EMTs.'"

"There has to be a piece we're missing," I say. "There's something we haven't thought of or we haven't found."

"Give the mistress a call," the detective tells me. "See what she has to say about all this. His impressive speech aside, there's something really suspicious about Ron McCain."

I end the call with Mason and take out the notebook to get Melissa Garrison's contact information. She answers on the second ring, a curious, uncertain note in her voice, like most people answering a call from a number they don't recognize.

"Melissa Garrison?" I ask.

"Yes," she says. "Who is this?"

"Hi, Ms. Garrison. My name is Dean Steele. I'm a private investigator."

"Private investigator?" She draws in a sharp breath. "This is about Erin, isn't it?"

"What do you mean?" I ask.

"Erin McCain," she says. "It's about her, isn't it? Is she alive? What happened to her?"

The words are coming out almost too fast for me to understand.

"I need you to slow down for just a second," I say. "Tell me what you're talking about."

"I'm sure you already know this, or you wouldn't be calling me, but I'm seeing a married man. His name is Ron McCain. We were spending time together the last couple of days, and he got an emergency call that his wife, Erin, was missing. He had to bring me home and leave very suddenly to find out if she's all right," she says. "Has she been found? Did something happen to her?"

"She has been found," I tell her. "And she is alive. But we need to focus on what you can tell me about Ron right now. You said that the two of you were spending some time together over the last couple of days. Can you tell me the circumstances of that?"

She draws in a shaky breath and lets it out slowly. "Ron had a business trip earlier this week. It was only for a couple of days, but he told Erin it was for the whole week. He went to the conference, but the last day was just some activities and things he said most of the people who go skip anyway, so he didn't go to them. Instead, he came to my place. Last night, he woke me up and said we should go on a little getaway for the last couple days that we were going to have together."

"A little getaway?" I ask.

"Yeah, I thought it was strange because we were already doing just fine at my place and we don't really do the taking trips together thing. I don't know what he told you about me, but we aren't really focused on the roses and violin music, if you catch my drift. We enjoy being together and have a lot of fun, but we are very aware of what we are and what we aren't, and we're not a vacationing couple. But he sounded really excited, and I thought it might be fun to get out of town for a day or two. Just something different to shake things up. I haven't been to the beach in a long time, and so it seemed like a good idea," she tells me. "Can you tell me what happened to Erin? He seemed so out of it when he left here I don't even know what's going on."

"I can't give you any details," I say. "What do you mean, he seemed out of it?"

"I'm not sure what was going on with him," she says. "We were at my house, and I fell asleep watching a movie. I must have been out for a couple of hours when he woke me up. He seemed really excited and energetic, like he just couldn't contain himself. He was already dressed and had packed his stuff up. He was taking clothes of mine out of the dresser and piling them up on the bed, telling me I should get packed because we were going to be spontaneous and take a trip.

"I'll admit I got swept up in it. That's the whole point of us seeing each other. Doing fun, crazy things together so that the rest of our lives are more interesting. I don't need to sit around and pay bills with a man. But I do like the excitement of rushing off in the middle of the night to some place fun. It was sexy and thrilling. But we'd only been at the hotel for a short time when his neighbor called him and told him that something was going on at his house and no one could find Erin. That's all he told me. We got packed up again and left. On the drive back to Briar Glen, he got another call that he needed to go to the hospital. He dropped me back off at my place and left. I haven't heard from him since."

"When you fell asleep, was Ron still awake?" I ask.

"I think so," she says. "Is he all right? He was so upset when he got those calls. He was so worried about her that he barely even said goodbye to me."

She sounds like she's attempting to defend him, but everything she says is only making me feel more suspicious of Ron McCain.

CHAPTER TWELVE

I need to speak with Erin McCain, but since that isn't an option right now, I have to go to the people around her in hopes that someone might have some information for me. It takes a little bit of searching, but I finally track down Meg Bower, Erin's volunteer supervisor. She's in her office with the door partially open when I get there. I knock on the door and peer inside to look at her.

"Hello," she says. "Can I help you?"

"Hi. My name is Dean Steele. I had your assistant call you to let you know I needed to speak with you," I say.

"The private investigator," she says, gesturing at the chair across the desk from where she's sitting. "Please, come in."

I close the door behind me and take the seat she indicated.

"Thank you for taking the time to talk to me," I say.

"Absolutely," she says. "What can I help you with?"

"I'm sure by now you've heard that Erin McCain is currently in the hospital being treated for injuries she sustained last night," I say.

"Oh," Meg says, shifting in her seat and taking off her glasses so she can briefly rub the bridge of her nose. "Yes, I have heard that. It's awful. Are you investigating what happened to her?"

"Yes," I say. "Right now, we still don't know exactly what happened or why. I'm hoping to find out more information about her and what was going on in her life so that I can have some direction to go on."

"Have you had a chance to speak with her husband?" she asks. "She mentioned to me earlier this week that he was going away on a business trip. She hated it when he was away. She always had trouble sleeping."

"He's actually here," I tell her. "We got in touch with him early this morning, and he was able to come back."

I'm not going to get into the full details about where he was or what he was doing. That information doesn't need to be spread around right now. It's going to come out. There's no getting around that. But like I told Ron, I'd like Erin to hear it from him before there's a chance of her finding out from someone else. I can't imagine the humiliation and hurt she would go through if she found out that her supervisor at her volunteer position knew her husband was cheating on her before she even got to know.

The thought of the secrets Ron was harboring brings my thoughts back to Joseph Palmer and Scott Russo and the horrible price they paid for the information they were holding on to. I can't help but wonder if what happened to Erin was related to her own husband's double life.

"That's good," she says. "What can I help you with?"

"Anything you can think of," I say. "Tell me about Erin McCain and what you know about her life."

She looks slightly baffled and sits back in her chair, looking off to the side like she's searching for an answer to give me.

"I'm not sure if I can be of any real help to you," she says. "I only knew her through her volunteering here at the hospital. She was—is—a fantastic volunteer. Very committed to everything she was doing and always willing to step in and do more when it's needed. If there's someone who needs help or she can think of a way to make the day better for a patient or the family member of a patient, she'll jump right in and do it. She really put all of herself into what she did here, and it was obvious how much she cared.

"When she applied to volunteer, I was the one who interviewed her, and she told me that her parents both spent a fairly considerable amount of time in the hospital before their deaths, and it was the people who she interacted with on a daily basis while she was spending time with them that made all the difference. Those people made it so much easier for her to go through something unimaginably hard, and she wanted to be that kind of force for someone else. I thought that was beautiful."

"It is," I say. "It takes a really special person to give of themselves that much. I am always impressed by people who have that much compassion and love for others inside them, no matter what they are facing."

"She's one of those really special ones," Meg confirms. "I hope so much that she is able to recover and we'll get her back. There will be a big hole here at the hospital for as long as she's gone."

"I'm sure there will be," I tell her. "Is there anything else you can think of? Did she have any problems going on in her life? Difficulties that she was having with other people?"

She shifts around again. It's obvious she's uncomfortable with this conversation, but she's one of the people with whom Erin spent a good amount of time, and I'm hoping that translated to her confiding in Meg if there was something going on in her life that might not have been immediately obvious to other people.

"I wouldn't know anything about that," she says. "Erin and I got along well, and she is a very sweet and wonderful person, but we weren't friends outside the hospital. We didn't spend time together other than when she was here for a shift."

"You said that she told you she hated when her husband was away and that she had trouble sleeping," I point out.

"That was only because one time when he was away, she seemed exhausted and out of it during a shift. I asked her about it because I was worried there was something really wrong, and she explained that her husband was out of town for work and she always had trouble sleeping when he wasn't home. Apparently, the night before that shift, he hadn't called her to say good night, and that made it even harder for her. He ended up calling her during the shift and explaining that he had been out with people for dinner and it turned into a much longer ordeal than he was expecting, but he didn't want to wake her up by calling her. She was relieved and happy after that," she says.

"And that's all you know?" I ask. "She never told you anything else about her personal life, her marriage, her friends, anyone who might have had a problem with her? You didn't know of anyone who might have had issues with her? Maybe one of the other volunteers?"

"No," she says. "She didn't confide in me that way. We were friendly when she was here, and I always enjoyed talking with her, but we didn't have that kind of relationship where she would open up to me about things going on in her life, if there was anything. But I never noticed her seeming particularly upset or distracted or anything. She always came in happy and ready to go. Except for that one time when she was so tired. There are days when she is less perky, of course, but even then, she was still friendly, upbeat, and optimistic.

"I don't remember a single time I saw her angry or saying a cross word to or about somebody, so I never had the need to ask her if anything was going wrong in her life. If I thought I needed to, I would have, and I'd like to think she would have trusted me enough to tell me if she was experiencing something serious, but we just haven't been the kind of people who chatted over coffee or shared our innermost thoughts."

I consider my next question for a few seconds before asking it.

"Has anyone spoken with you about Sophie Berman?" I ask.

She looks confused. "Sophie? No, I..." Her face suddenly goes red, and her eyes widen. "She's the sister of the nurse. The one who died this morning."

"Yes," I say.

"She wasn't supposed to come in today, so I didn't think about it. No one said her name, just that the sister of one of the nurses died this morning and he had to leave work. I can't believe I didn't know."

"I'm sorry no one came to tell you directly," I say. "Right now, things are very much up in the air when it comes to her death, and we are doing our best to figure it out."

"You don't know what happened to her?" she asks.

"We don't know the details," I say. "Do you know anything about Sophie's life that might be applicable? Anything that you knew about her or something she might have been going through that could lead us in a new direction?"

"No," she says, shaking her head and sniffling as if the news of Sophie's death has compounded talking about Erin's attack and overwhelmed her. "I maintained the same kind of friendly professionalism with her that I did with Erin. She was a good volunteer, too. Not like Erin. She wasn't quite as effervescent, but still very good and helpful. There were a couple of times when I thought she seemed upset, but if I asked if she was all right, she would smile and say she was fine. Nothing out of the ordinary or more than other people I've worked with before."

"Did you know the two of them were friends?" I ask.

"I saw them talking during their shifts together, and they seemed friendly," she says.

"All right. Thank you for your time. I'll get back in touch with you if I think of anything else. And please call me if you do," I say, handing her one of my cards.

"I will," she says. "Thank you for coming to talk to me."

As I leave the office, I see her staring at the card in her hand. She looks stunned, and I can't blame her. This is a lot to process, even for someone who admits to not knowing the women very well beyond what she needed to for their volunteer positions at the hospital.

I walk out of the hospital and head for my car. I drive to the police department and call Detective Cartwright when I pull into the parking lot. He meets me at the door and brings me back to where he's set up a war room for the case.

"Did you find out anything else?" he asks when we've settled into the room with ice water.

"I talked to Ron McCain's mistress, Melissa Garrison, and she told me pretty much the same thing that he did about their relationship. Neither one of them looks at it like some dramatic romance, and there are no intentions of them being a real couple at any point. From the beginning, they agreed not to consider that they would ever have a future together, and it was understood that Ron wants to stay with his wife and does not want anything to compromise their relationship. He never meant for Erin to find out about the affair and only looked at it as a way to add some excitement to his life," he says.

"That seems like a hell of a leap," Cartwright says. "You want some excitement in your life, you go skydiving or do a NASCAR ride experience. You don't find a girlfriend."

"That's about what I was thinking when he told me," I say. "But Melissa had the same thoughts. She said they enjoy being together and everything, but she doesn't want to have any kind of commitment to anyone, much less Ron. She was even surprised when he suggested that they go on a getaway together because that seemed too romantic for the two of them."

"Too romantic?" he asks.

I nod. "It is what it is. That's not the main point. She told me that she fell asleep while they were watching a movie and that when Ron woke her up to suggest they head off on this spontaneous getaway together, he was really worked up and excited. She even made a point to say that he was already dressed, which suggested to me that he wasn't when she fell asleep. Melissa was really upset about what's going on with Erin and said that Ron was too, but that still strikes me as very odd.

"After I talked to her, I went to see the volunteer coordinator. She gushed about what an amazing volunteer Erin is but said that they weren't on a very personal basis. They were friendly rather than friends, essentially," I say.

"So she didn't know anything about her life or the people in it," Mason says.

"Exactly. Other than saying that, she noticed her exhausted one day and found out that she doesn't sleep well when her husband is away on business. Which makes me wonder, how much of the time when he says he's away on business is it actually business? How much sleep is she losing over this affair without even knowing it?"

"An interesting question to ponder," he says. "But we don't know if it has anything to do with this case. He might be a sleazebag and a terrible husband, but that doesn't necessarily make him a murderer. Right now, we still have two missing EMTs and a death we can't explain. What would any of that have to do with Ron McCain having a girlfriend on the side?"

"I don't know," I say. "It's something to keep in mind, but we have to move forward with something else."

"Exactly what I was thinking. Sylvia Carruthers mentioned that she saw a police car in the driveway at one point when she was looking at the house, but then when she went over there, it wasn't there anymore. We still haven't been able to confirm that there was a car there or why it would be there, or anything about the ambulance being called out to the scene. I'm going to keep looking into that. I thought you could go and speak with the neighbors. See if any of them noticed something other than what Sylvia told us," he tells me.

"I'm on it," I say.

I finish off the water and head out of the police department, starting to feel the long day dragging on me. Suspicions are starting to build up, but there are still too many missing pieces to this puzzle. I'm hoping talking to the neighbors might shed light on something and get us closer to the answers.

CHAPTER THIRTEEN

The cars are gone from the McCain house, but pieces of the crime scene tape still cling in some places around the house. Ron will have to face it when he comes home. I know Erin's blood is still inside the kitchen. He'll see it on the floor and on the counter. Then up in the attic, he'll have to confront the far more intense scene of where Sophie's body lay.

Having to come face-to-face with the scene of a crime after it happened just furthers the trauma of going through something like this with a loved one, but it's a necessary evil. The investigative units and first responders don't clean up the scene. They investigate and search it as much as they need and then leave behind what's left for those still using the scene to handle. Ron will either have to clean up the blood in the attic himself or contact a crime scene cleanup unit that can come and fix it for him. Either way, it will only make the situation more difficult, as he has to contend with the fact of his home not being a place of peace and respite.

I park in Kent and Sylvia's driveway and take my notebook as I go over to the house next to Erin and Ron's. It's getting to the middle of the afternoon, but I'm not sure if anyone will answer. The people living in the house may be at work. That seems to be the case, as they don't answer the door. I tuck my business card into the door and hope that they get in touch with me. I move on to the house on the other side. A woman answers the door quickly enough that it almost seems like she's been watching me and expecting the ring of her doorbell.

"Can I help you?" she says, looking out at me through a small gap in the door she holds mostly closed in front of her.

"Hi," I say. "My name is Dean Steele. I'm a private investigator. Are you aware of an incident happening at the house two down earlier this morning?"

"A private investigator?" she asks.

"Yes. I'm working with the police to investigate what happened at the home of Ron and Erin McCain. Do you know them?" I ask.

"Yes," she says. "They are good people."

"Did you know that something happened at their house today?" I ask.

"I heard the sirens. But I don't know any of the details."

"So you didn't see anything happening or hear anything unusual prior to hearing the police and ambulance arrive?" I ask.

"No, I'm a heavy sleeper. I didn't know anything was happening until I was already up making breakfast and heard all the hubbub out there. What happened?" she asks.

"I can't share any details right now," I tell her. "I'm collecting information that I hope will help the investigation uncover exactly what happened."

"I'm sorry I can't be any more help," she says.

"That's all right. Thank you for your time." I hand her one of my cards. "If you do happen to think of something, even if it doesn't seem like it means anything, please give me a call. I'm staying right across the street in Kent and Sylvia's house, so I am easy to get hold of if you need to speak with me."

"Kent and Sylvia?" she asks.

"I'm an old friend of Kent's," I explain.

She nods and steps back. "Have a nice afternoon."

I go to the next house down the line, and a man comes to the door. He looks like he's just gotten home from work or is preparing to leave for some sort of work function in a suit, without the jacket but with a firmly knotted tie and highly polished shoes.

"Hello," he says.

I introduce myself the same way I did to the first neighbor.

"Benjamin Grier," he says, reaching out a hand.

He gives me a firm handshake and steps out onto the porch with me. It's more welcoming than the first neighbor hiding behind her door, but I'm still standing with the intense sunlight shining on the back of my neck. I'm glad for the temperature not being as high as it has been the last few days.

"Mr. Grier, are you aware there was an incident in the house a few doors down early this morning?" I ask.

"Yes," he says. "I was planning on sleeping in a little today, but the sound of the sirens woke me up. I looked out there and saw the police and ambulances at the McCain house. I was really curious about what happened and have been watching the news, but there hasn't been anything yet."

"Information isn't being shared quite yet," I tell him. "There might be something on the news this evening. You said that the sirens woke you, so you didn't hear or see anything before that? You didn't notice the lights of an ambulance before that or hear car doors or people or anything?"

"No, my bedroom window doesn't point toward the front of their house, so the lights wouldn't have gotten to me. I sleep with a fan on, which blocks out sounds that aren't really loud. The sirens were loud enough to get over it, but things like voices and regular cars and things are drowned out by it. Have you spoken with the Cumberlands yet?" he asks.

I shake my head. "Who are they?"

"They live across the street." He points to a house.

"Next door to Kent and Sylvia Carruthers?" I ask.

"Yeah," he says. "I chatted with Keith Cumberland earlier today, and he asked if I'd heard everything going on early this morning. He mentioned that he'd seen the first ambulance there a long time before the second one came and was wondering what was going on. I didn't know they came at different times, so I didn't have anything to tell him, but you might want to talk to him. He could have seen or heard something else."

"Thank you. I appreciate it. One more thing. Do you know the McCains?" I ask.

"I know them as neighbors," he says. "I wouldn't say we're good friends, but we've talked at block parties and open houses and things around the neighborhood."

"So you wouldn't know if they were experiencing any kind of trouble with anyone," I say.

"No."

"All right, thank you." I give him a card like I did with the first neighbor and head across the street.

Miranda Cumberland answers the door and calls for her husband after I introduce myself, reminding her that we met briefly when Kent and I were sitting outside a couple of days ago. He comes to the door in jeans and a T-shirt, glazed with sweat. He wipes his hands on a bandanna in his back pocket the way I did when I was helping Kent out with the projects around the house.

"Sorry," he says, looking at his hands to make sure they are clean before reaching out to shake mine. "I was working in the backyard."

"No problem," I say. "Sorry to interrupt you. I just wanted to talk to the two of you about what happened across the street early this morning. I'm helping the police investigate and am canvassing neighbors to find out anything that anyone might have seen or heard that could have something to do with what happened. Benjamin across the street told me the two of you talked today and you told him you saw the first ambulance at the house."

"That's right," Keith says. "I was walking my dog this morning and noticed the lights before I even got out of the house. They were shining in through the window in the living room, and I thought that was really strange. When I went outside, I saw the ambulance sitting outside the McCain house. I was worried, but I also thought it was really strange because the stretcher was sitting out in the road and no one was around it. I took my dog on our usual walk around the neighborhood, and when we got back, everything was still the way that it had been."

"Did you see Sylvia Carruthers when you came back?" I ask, trying to get a timeline going in my head.

"No," he says. "The neighborhood was really quiet. I think most people were still asleep. But Boomer likes to walk early."

"Did you notice anything else when you saw the police? Did you hear anything around the house?" I ask.

"No," he says, shaking his head. "But this morning I was woken up by something. I didn't know exactly what it was, but something woke me out of a dead sleep. Miranda said she thought it sounded like a scream."

"A scream?" I ask. "What kind of scream?"

"I don't really know that it was a scream," Miranda says. "It woke me up too. But there was just the impression that I'd heard someone screaming, and it woke me up. But then it was quiet after that. And when Keith came home, he told me that he saw the ambulance, and I figured that maybe it wasn't a scream but the siren of that ambulance. When we heard the police sirens and the other ambulance, it made me think that it was that rather than actual screaming."

"Did you go over to the house or anything to see what might be going on when you noticed the ambulance?" I ask Keith.

"No, I didn't go over to the house, but I did call both Ron and Erin McCain to check on them and see if there was anything I could do. Neither of them answered their phones. I decided that the whole situation really wasn't any of my business and if they needed me for anything, they would let me know. I just went home and went back to bed for a while. I was just glad that whatever was going on, help was there for them. Later, when the other ambulance and the police got there, it seemed really weird, but I didn't know what to do," he says.

"What happened?" Miranda asks. "Are they all right?"

"I can't share any details right now," I say. "But more information should be available soon. Thank you for your help. I'm still over at Kent and Sylvia's place, so if you can think of anything else that might be important, don't hesitate to come talk to me."

As I'm walking away from the house, I notice Bill Meyer, the police officer who came over earlier. He's in his driveway looking through his car, and I notice his squad car parked beside it. Jogging across the street, I call out to him.

"Hey, Bill."

He backs out of the car and looks over at me, waving when he recognizes me.

"Hey, Dean," he says. "How's everything?"

He's not asking about me. He wants to check in with the investigation, which I fully understand. He isn't involved in the official investigation, which has to be frustrating considering he was there at the very beginning. He was there when Erin McCain was found but hasn't been a part of everything that has happened since.

"Erin has been sedated and is being kept in the hospital for now," I tell him. "Ron got back and is with her. The doctor says she is responding well to treatment so far, and they will determine when they can safely bring her out of sedation so we can talk to her."

"That's good," he says.

"I'm just here talking to the neighbors to see if anyone noticed anything when the first ambulance was here. It seems like most people slept through the first ambulance getting here, and while it was here, but then woke up after we called dispatch and the police and ambulance came.

Keith Cumberland said he saw the first ambulance while he was walking his dog and tried to call both of the McCains but didn't get an answer."

I decide not to tell him about Ron's affair and where he actually was when Kent called him this morning. That is a fallout that Ron is going to have to deal with at some point, but it's not up to me to start that happening.

"It was very odd to see that ambulance sitting out in front of the house with no one around it," Bill says.

I give him a quizzical look. According to both Sylvia and him, he didn't come over until after she was already there and I was inside the house. My eyes move over to the squad car. He follows my look, and something flickers across his eyes like he realizes what he said.

"Bill, is your squad car always parked in your driveway?" I ask.

He hesitates, looking like he's trying to decide what he's going to say. Finally, his shoulders drop, and his expression goes to regret.

"It was my car," he says. "I know that's what you're thinking, and you're right. It was my car that Sylvia saw in the driveway when she looked outside."

"You were parked in the McCain driveway?" I ask. "Did you go inside the house?"

"No," he says. "I didn't even get out of my car. My shift was over, and when I was coming home, I saw the ambulance sitting outside the McCain house. It was just sitting there with the stretcher out in the street. The door was open, but there wasn't anyone around it or coming out of the house. I didn't hear anything. It just struck me as weird, and I wanted to check and make sure everything was okay. I pulled into the driveway and was going to go inside, but then my wife called. I'd already let her know that I was on my way, and she was feeling sick, so I wanted to get home to her.

"No dispatch had come through that the McCain house needed help, and I noticed it wasn't one of the main services' ambulances, so I figured something relatively minor was going on and that they had it under control. I knew Ron was away for business and thought maybe Erin had fallen or was feeling sick. Something that would require some help, but not the police. I didn't want to get involved when I didn't know what was going on. So I left. I shouldn't have. I should have gotten involved and not just come over later when I saw Sylvia out there."

"Why didn't you say anything when she was talking about seeing the car in the driveway?" I ask.

"I knew how bad it looked," he admitted. "I could have responded to the situation and possibly stopped whatever was happening, but I didn't. I decided to stay out of it, and something horrific happened. I didn't want that coming down on me."

He looks like he feels terrible about the whole situation, and frankly, he should. This is completely unacceptable. Unfortunately, there's really nothing I can do about it. What he did isn't illegal, and it's unlikely he would even face consequences at work because of it. I'll make sure to tell Detective Cartwright so that loose end is tied up and we stop trying to follow it, but for now, I'm angry.

"You didn't want to admit that you just left a scene?" I say. "You didn't do anything illegal or even something you were obligated to do, but you obviously thought there was something wrong enough that you were compelled to pull into that driveway. When you found out that Sylvia saw your car and we were wondering who it was, you should have said something. Time has been wasted trying to track down the mysterious police officer who we were worried could be missing, like the EMTs."

"I'm sorry," he says. "I know I should have done something, but I didn't want to admit I just drove away."

My phone rings in my pocket, and I pull it out.

"Hey, Detective," I answer.

"I have some more information. How has talking to the neighbors gone?" Detective Cartwright asks.

"I have a few bits of information for you too," I say, eyeing Bill, who looks embarrassed.

"Come on back, and we'll talk it through," he says.

"Be there in a few minutes."

Without another word to Bill, I cross the street and get back in my car.

CHAPTER FOURTEEN

MASON IS WAITING FOR ME IN THE INVESTIGATION ROOM when I get to the police department. I notice new files sitting on the table and hope they contain something valuable.

"What did you find out from the neighbors?" he immediately asks when I get into the room.

"I only got to talk to a few of them. The first couple of people I talked to didn't have anything to add. They completely slept through the first ambulance arriving and didn't even know anything was going on until later, when the police and the other ambulance arrived. They were really interested in finding out what happened to the McCains though. One of them suggested I go talk to the people living next door to the Carruthers, Sylvia and Kent."

"The woman who was there at the scene?" Mason confirms.

"Yeah and her husband. The one who called Ron McCain to let him know what was going on with Erin. I went to their neighbor, and he said that he had to walk his dog really early in the morning and noticed the

THE WOMAN IN THE ATTIC

ambulance sitting outside with the stretcher on the street. He thought it was really odd and was worried about the couple, so he called them, but they didn't answer. He decided it wasn't any of his business, as he put it, and went back to the house, but then he noticed the first responders and everything going on later. One thing that was interesting is that he and his wife mentioned that they heard something that woke them up before he needed to walk the dog, and she thought it was a scream," I say.

"A scream? Like a person screaming?" the detective asks.

"Yes. But then when they saw the ambulance, they thought it was possibly the sound of a siren that had actually woken them up. Keith said that everything was quiet when he was out with the dog, and he didn't see or hear anything unusual other than the ambulance itself. And that brings me to Bill Meyer," I say.

One eyebrow lifts. "Bill Meyer? Officer Bill Meyer?"

"Who lives next door to the McCains? That would be the one. He finally admitted it was his police car sitting in the driveway that Sylvia saw and then was missing when we went over there. He said that he pulled into the driveway when he was coming home from his shift and saw the ambulance. He thought that something might be happening, but then his wife called him and wasn't feeling well, so he decided not to get himself involved in whatever was going on at the house. The ambulance was already there, so he figured that they had everything under control and if they needed additional help, they'd let him know. He just didn't want anyone to know it was him."

"I'm going to have to have a talk with him," Detective Cartwright says.

"I thought you might," I say. "But the general overriding theme about everything I heard from the neighbors was about that ambulance. I really think we need to find out more about it and the EMTs who were there. They seem to be at the center of this."

"Good to hear you say that because the information I have to share with you is about the ambulance," he says.

"What did you find out?" I ask.

"We ran the VIN on the ambulance and found out that it was purchased at an auction several years ago. Since then it has been through a few different owners, but the last one it was registered to died last year. His children sold it through an online marketplace but didn't follow through to make sure that the registration was changed. Since the owner died only a few weeks after renewing the registration, there's been nothing to make them think something was wrong. When I spoke with his son, he admitted they rushed through getting rid of their father's stuff because he was a bit of a hoarder and had so much random junk," he says.

"Like an old ambulance," I say.

"Exactly," he says.

"And I'm assuming that they didn't know who they sold it to," I say.

"They said they erased all the communications about the sale because they were through email and didn't think they would need them. He remembers the name Nathan Guthrie because he could have sworn it was a country music singer. I kid you not, those were his words."

"Well, thank goodness for names sticking because of misunderstandings," I say. "But they didn't get any proof?"

"No, I have some people investigating the Nathan Guthrie name, but I don't think they're going to come up with anything. Someone who doesn't register a vehicle after purchasing it isn't going to give their real name when they are buying it," he says.

"I have a feeling you're right about that," I say.

"We do have something more concrete, though." He flips open one of the files, revealing images of tire impressions made in ink across several pages. "We took these from the tires. It doesn't help us right this second, but if we're able to find these impressions somewhere else, it could link the ambulance to people."

"Can we go look at the ambulance?" I ask.

"Sure," he says. "It's being kept at a storage unit for now until it's fully cleared."

We go down to the ambulance, and Detective Cartwright uses a tagged key to open the back so we can climb inside. The heat has made it feel like an oven inside, and I leave the doors open for a few seconds to air out the damp, hot inside before climbing in. I look around, taking it in. It's obviously not a vehicle intended to support life or provide intense medical care for someone. There are blood pressure cuff and a stretcher, first aid supplies, and a tank of oxygen with a mask, but nothing else. I pick up one of the blankets again.

"What is this?" I ask, showing the detective the logo on the corner.

"I don't know," he says.

"We need to find out."

I get out of the back of the ambulance and go around to the passenger door so I can dig through the front cabin. I'm hoping to find something useful, like receipts, but there are no papers or bits of trash. There's a pair of sunglasses and a box of surgical masks, nothing else. I get out and close the door, shaking my head.

"Whoever was in this thing kept it clean and didn't leave anything behind," I say.

We go back inside and into the investigation room, where he opens a computer. He takes a picture of the logo at the corner of the blanket and runs it through a search.

"Look," he says, pointing at the screen. "It's from an old hospital."

"An old hospital?" I ask, walking around to his side so I can lean in and look at the screen.

The search has brought up a listing for a hospital in the next town that has been closed down for several years. The logo is the same as the sign outside the hospital and all the pages of the defunct website.

"So a fake ambulance had blankets from a hospital that hasn't been operational in years," Mason says.

"Whoever owns it could easily have bought the blankets at a surplus sale, like they bought the ambulance at the auction. When a place like that closes, they liquidate everything in it, so that could have happened with the blankets, but this is all really fucking strange," I say.

I'm still worried about the EMT that Erin has been asking about, but now that worry is mixed with heavy, dragging suspicion. Something isn't right. The pieces aren't fitting together, and I don't know what to think.

"I know it's getting late," Mason says. "But how do you feel about a field trip?"

"To the hospital?" I ask.

"I think we need to have a look at it. These blankets are in there for a reason. Whether it's just that they were bought because they were cheap and looked medical, or something else, we need to find out."

"Absolutely," I say.

"Let's go," I say.

We take the detective's car and follow the GPS to the old hospital. It's set outside of town, leaving it looking desolate and foreboding. A large fence was constructed around the perimeter at one point, likely soon after it was closed, but the lock on the gate is broken, and the gate is standing open by several feet. I get out of the car and open the gate the rest of the way to allow the car through, and we drive slowly up toward the building.

We are clearly not the first people to venture to the hospital since it was closed. The building has been ravaged by time, and people have come to turn it into their own playground. Once ornamental trees have become overgrown, and vines have formed on the walls. Graffiti mars the brick, and several of the windows I see are broken. The vast parking lot, now lined with veins of grass and small trees, is eerie, stretched out in the growing dusk. Lights, still on the grid for safety and insurance purposes, have turned on, glowing on the empty spots and revealing more of the broken pavement.

We pull up directly in front of what was once the main entrance to the hospital. I think of earlier today when I was going inside Briar Glen General and saw Ron racing toward the door to get to his wife. Those were the last moments before the suspicion set in, the last minutes before I found out what was right under the surface, complicating the already twisted and confusing case. Now we're at the hunkering carcass of a former hospital, waiting to find out what might be inside that could shed light on the strange happenings at the McCain house.

Approaching the doors, we see that they are covered with plyboard that is chained and padlocked into place. A couple of places look like they have been pulled on by someone trying to yank the boards away but weren't successful. Cartwright and I walk around the perimeter of the building, seeing if there are any indications that people have gotten inside. I have no doubt that they have. A building like this left to rot in the middle of nowhere is irresistible to many types of people.

Finally, we find a side door that has a broken chain. Cartwright takes out his flashlight, and I pull out my phone, bringing up the flashlight feature, so that we can get as much light inside as we can. He opens the door, and we pause for a moment, waiting to hear anything that might come from the inside. When there's nothing, we enter cautiously. I stop just inside the door, shining the light around myself and taking in my surroundings.

The damp warmth inside the building is a stark contrast to the cold that usually permeates hospitals. There is no sharp smell of cleaners or sound of machinery. Everything is still and quiet. We move further into the hospital and see all that's left behind when the facility closed. There are still chairs scattered around the waiting area. I see a few pamphlets and brochures stacked on what used to be the information desk.

Unsure of exactly what we're looking for, we continue on. From deeper into the building, I hear a sound, but I'm not sure what it is. Cartwright seems to have heard it too and turns his flashlight in the direction of it.

"Briar Glen Police," he announces himself. "Anyone who is inside, make yourself known."

There's no response or movement. He takes out his gun as we walk further, finding ourselves in a suite of offices. There's evidence here that people have been spending a lot of time in these offices. There are sleeping bags and pillows, and the corners of the rooms are piled with belongings and trash. We go through each of the rooms that are unlocked or that have been broken into, but we don't find anyone. Either they have moved on from this space or are out during the day looking for food and money.

With the bottom floor of the hospital cleared, we go up the stairwell to the second floor. Here there are patient rooms along the hallways, some of them still outfitted with the beds and other features that would have been there when this place was operational. I go into one of the rooms and find a blanket balled up at the foot of the bed. It looks like the one from the ambulance.

"Either they bought brand-new blankets that hadn't come here from a surplus sale or they stole used ones, because it looks like quite a few are still here," I point out.

"It looks like a lot is still here," Cartwright says. "Like they just walked out one day, closed the door, and didn't look back. It's really freaking eerie."

"It is," I say. "Do you want to keep looking?"

He nods. "A little further."

We continue on, and I hear a shuffling noise. I can't place where it came from, but it makes the detective stop too. We listen for a few seconds but don't hear anything else. He walks on toward the next patient room, and as I'm starting to follow him, a figure lunges out of the room beside me and latches an arm around my neck. I drop my phone and clutch at the arm, shouting at Cartwright as the person drags me backward into the room and kicks the door shut.

The board that was put over the window in this room was taken down, allowing some of the evening light from outside to filter in, but it's still dark. I can't see what's in front of me or who has me. The door opens as I swing my arm back and plant my elbow in the person's stomach. They pitch forward, and their grip on me loosens, allowing me to move away from them, but they immediately run at me again.

"This is my place!" the man shouts. "It's mine! What are you doing here?"

Cartwright stands at the door with his gun poised, but there's little he can do. I bend forward and wrap both arms around his waist, pushing him back toward the bed.

"Briar Glen Police! Stop what you're doing!" Cartwright commands from the doorway.

"This place is mine!" he repeats.

I get him into the bed and pin him down with my knee to his stomach and my hands on his wrists.

"It's mine!"

"Stop fighting!" I tell him. "We're not here to hurt you."

"I told the others! I told them all! The doctor, the nurses, everyone. I told them. This is mine, and they can't have it!"

He's still trying to thrash, but the man is smaller than me, so he doesn't have the power to force me off. He continues to rant about this being his place and him telling everyone, becoming more incoherent the more he says.

I look back at Mason.

"We need to get him to the hospital," I say. "I think he needs some attention."

Mason helps me get the man in handcuffs and explains to him that we're going to bring him somewhere to get some help. He isn't pleased with this announcement and tries to get away from us, but with each of us controlling one side, we guide him back along the same path we took to the car and put him in the back.

"That wasn't what I was expecting to find in there," Cartwright says to me as we're pulling away from the hospital.

"What were you expecting?" I ask.

"I don't know," he says. "But I was hoping for something."

"It's my place," the man says from the back of the car, an ominous tinge to the edges of the words. "I told them all."

CHAPTER FIFTEEN

WE GET THE MAN TO THE HOSPITAL AND BRING HIM INTO the emergency room. He refuses to tell us his name, so we register him as a John Doe and explain the situation to the doctor who comes in. They tell us they will check him over and set him up with a psychiatric evaluation to determine what the next steps should be. They will have him at the hospital for at least three days, so we wish him luck, say our goodbyes, and leave him muttering about the closed hospital and our invasion.

Since we are already here, we go up to the fourth floor to check on Erin McCain. The doctor who took over from Dr. Bishop, a younger woman named Dr. Merryweather, tells us that her condition is the same. She also tells us that Ron sat with her all day up until just recently, when they sent him home to get some rest. He told them he would be back tomorrow morning. They don't have a set plan yet of when they will bring her out of the sedation, but they promise to keep us updated.

As we're leaving the hospital, I turn to Detective Cartwright.

"What's next? Back to the department?" I ask.

"What's next is getting some rest, just like they told Ron," he tells me. "It's getting late, and you've been going at this all day. You need to get some real food in you and get some sleep."

"But there are still two people missing," I say. "And a suspicious death."

"And we'll start back up first thing in the morning," he says. "We can't let you get totally burned out the first day of the investigation."

"I don't get burned out," I tell him.

"I've heard that. But I don't want this to be the case that tests that theory. Go back to where you're staying and take a load off for a while. Meet me at the station tomorrow morning, and we'll dive back in. And, Dean," he says, making direct eye contact with me, "remember, I know your reputation. Don't go back to that hospital without me."

He knew exactly what I was thinking, and I'm disappointed to have to confirm to him that I won't go back and continue the search on my own.

"There could still be something there," I point out.

"And we'll have a team clear the entire thing tomorrow. For now, both of us are going to get some rest and regroup. I'll see you tomorrow."

He heads for his car, and I hesitate for a second before making my way to mine. He's right. It is late, and I've been working on this case since very early this morning. I'm tired and hungry, but I still have the adrenaline of an open case and haunting questions lingering over me. I don't want to stop yet. I don't have the choice, though, so I drive back to Kent and Sylvia's house.

I use the spare key I haven't returned to them yet to let myself into the house. I smell the rich scent of tomato sauce and garlic bread, and my stomach rumbles even more. I'm hungrier than I even realized.

"Dean?" Kent calls from the kitchen.

"Hey," I call out. "Yeah, it's me."

"Just in time. Dinner is ready."

I walk into the kitchen and breathe in the wonderful smells again.

"It smells amazing."

Kent grins as he takes thick pieces of garlic bread off a hot pan and puts them in a bread basket on the counter. He hands it to me.

"Can you put that on the table for me?"

"Sure."

I take the basket and bring it into the dining room, where an enormous bowl of salad is already waiting at the center of the table. I set the basket down and go back into the kitchen to see if there's anything else I can do to help. Sylvia is ladling the thick sauce over a bowl of pasta and tossing it around while Kent collects the silverware and napkins. I help set the table, and we're finally sitting ready to eat. I'm ravenous by the time the bowl of salad gets into my hands, and I serve up a mound into my own bowl before drizzling it with dressing and diving in.

Kent laughs. "Didn't get a chance to stop for food much today, did you?" he asks.

I slow down and finish chewing. "Sorry, not really."

"Don't apologize. I'm glad you're back here and actually eating," Sylvia says. "I've been worried about you all day."

"What happened today?" Kent asks. "Is Erin doing all right? We saw on the news that she was found in the woods and is in pretty serious condition."

He adds that last part like he wants to make sure that I know he isn't prying too deep, that there is already some information out there and he just wants my perspective on it.

"She's at the hospital under sedation," I tell them. "Ron spent most of the day with her once he got back."

Sylvia nods. "I saw him getting back to his house not too long before you got here. I wanted to talk to him, but I didn't know what to say. I have no idea how to handle a situation like this."

"I don't think many people do," I say. "It's not something you prepare for."

"Did you get a chance to talk to him?" Kent asks.

I nod. "I did. I know you haven't been living here long, so you aren't all that close yet, but did you ever notice any problems between the two of them? Did you ever hear them arguing or see anything that was suspicious?"

This isn't exactly dinner conversation, but as long as I have the two of them here, I might as well ask them what they may know. I have a feeling they are going to be some of the first to find out about the affair, so I'm curious if they know anything now.

They look at each other and then back at me.

"No," Kent says. "They always seemed good. I mean, like you said, we really didn't know them all that well yet. We're getting to know them, and I consider them friends, but we're not quite at that place where they'd confide in us about marital problems if they were having them or anything."

"But you didn't see anything that you would think meant they were having problems?" I ask.

"Not really. I mean, there were a couple of times when he left for business trips or something and she didn't walk him out to the car, but I don't think that's like a huge red flag indicating they were on their way to divorce court or anything," Sylvia says. Her eyes suddenly get wide. "Do you think he did this to her? Is he a suspect?"

"No one is a suspect right now," I say. "And it's not that I think he did anything. I'm just trying to understand everything going on from all angles."

"What about that weird ambulance?" Kent asks. "Sylvia saw it really early this morning, and it was just there for hours. When did you notice it?"

"When I was putting my stuff in the car to leave," I tell him. "Speaking of which, I don't know how long this investigation is going to last or how long I'm going to need to be in town. I really don't want to impose on you, so it's perfectly fine with me to go stay in a hotel."

"Don't be ridiculous," Sylvia says.

"You're staying here for as long as you need to," Kent says. "I'm glad to have you around, even if it is under these circumstances."

"Thanks," I say. "That makes things a lot easier and a lot more comfortable for me. I really appreciate it."

"Of course," Kent says. "But anyway, did you find out anything about the ambulance or about the EMTs?"

"That's right," Sylvia says. "I didn't even think about them. I've been so worried thinking about Erin and so upset about that woman you found…"

"Sophie Berman," I tell her.

"She was on the news too," Kent says. "It said the cause of death wasn't being released."

"We haven't heard from the medical examiner yet," I tell him. "Right now, it's just the information that we have from what we saw at the scene, but we're not going to reveal that to the public. I talked to her brother and searched her apartment, but I didn't find anything that seemed to have anything to do with her death. Her brother, Carson, did tell me that they were friends. That's as much as he knows, though. He hasn't really interacted with Erin much.

"As for the ambulance, that is still something we're investigating and trying to figure out. There are some details I can't share with you, but I'll tell you that it's a very strange situation. No ambulance was dispatched to their address until we called. We haven't had the chance to look at their phones to see if either of them called for a private service, but the detective wasn't even able to identify it as being one of the private fleets that he knows about. We haven't found any leads about the missing EMTs. Erin was talking about them when we found her, saying one of them was helping her and that she was worried about him, but that's all we have."

We fall into silence as we continue eating and gradually change the subject to talking about their days. When we're finished, we clear the table, and Sylvia brings out a strawberry and cream trifle that she sets on the table.

"Anyone want some decaf to go with their dessert?" she asks.

Both of us take her up on the officer, and Kent starts dishing up large portions of the luscious-looking layers of cream, strawberries, and cake into glass bowls.

"It's nice outside. Let's eat our dessert on the porch," he suggests when Sylvia comes back with a tray filled with coffee mugs, cream, and sugar.

He picks up his bowl and one for Sylvia, and we go out onto the front porch that he and I finished a couple of days ago. I sit on the top step as they take the swing, and we savor the cool night as we enjoy our dessert.

A few bites in, Sylvia looks across the street toward the McCain house. There are a couple of lights on inside, and the pieces of police tape have been taken down. Ron is trying to get back to normal. I can't help but wonder about the blood in the attic and if he has even gone up to face it yet.

"You know, I heard a story from a friend once about a strange ambulance," she says without looking away from the house.

"What story?" I ask.

She turns to me. "It wasn't too long ago, actually. A couple of months, maybe? She told me that she heard that some woman disappeared after being taken away in an ambulance."

I perk up, intrigued. "Who was it? What happened to her?"

"I don't know," Sylvia says. "She didn't have any other details. She just said she'd heard about a woman being taken away in an ambulance and then never being seen again. I want to say there was a news story about a woman being missing right around that time, too, but I don't really remember."

The story sticks with me as I finish dessert and go upstairs for a much-needed shower. Without details, it's harder to really follow through with something like that, but it's enough to further emphasize my suspicion about the ambulance and whoever was inside.

I get ready for bed and call to check in with Xavier. Nicole answers the video call. She looks tired and just a touch on edge.

"Hey, Nicole," I say. "How are you doing?"

"I'm tired, Dean. Four days of this is enough for anybody," she says. "Do you know what kind of nonsense that man has in his storage rooms? Yes, rooms. With an *s*. We've only gotten through one and are on the second one, and I think it might be better to just advertise the house as coming with its own treasure hunt and leave it at that."

"I thought you were ready to do battle," I say.

"That was before I discovered the very fun game of 'What the Hell Is This?' that we get to play while going through all these boxes. And steamer trunks. Steamer trunks, Dean. Who owns steamer trunks?" she asks.

"I mean… Xavier," I say.

"This is true," she says. "I probably shouldn't be so surprised by it, all considering."

"Where is he?" I ask, somewhat worried that she just left him in one of the storage rooms unattended and he has now taken to organizing things by size and color.

But just as I ask, Xavier zips past behind her. His speed and the smoothness of his movement are a bit jarring.

"There," she says. He zips past in the other direction. "And now there."

"What is he doing?"

"That would be roller-skating," she says. "He discovered his old pair of skates and has been skating around the house since dinner. I don't know if he's just rusty or if he's doing roller derby in his head, but he flipped over the couch at one point and almost took out the lamp."

"I can honestly tell you, I have no idea," I say. "I've seen him ice-skate, and it wasn't great."

I think back to when he went skating with Cupcake and clung to her the entire time. It looked really sweet from the perspective of people casually watching, but I knew it was because he was trying to keep his feet under him. The fact that Xavier owns roller skates would suggest that he has at least some skill with them, but again, this is Xavier. There's no actual telling why he has them in the first place.

Xavier glides to a stop beside Nicole, and his face appears beside hers on the screen.

"Hey, Dean," he says, sounding out of breath. "I found my roller skates."

"I heard. I also heard you flipped over the couch," I say.

"Miscalculation," he says. "Roller derby."

"And there's your answer," I say to Nicole. She shoves the phone into Xavier's hand. "I'm going to take a shower. Don't fall over while I'm gone."

THE WOMAN IN THE ATTIC

"Are you okay?" Xavier asks when she's gone. "Nicole said you called earlier to say you couldn't come home today."

"I got involved in a case," I tell him. "The detective handling it asked me to help him, and so I might be a while longer. If you want to come and stay here with me at any point, you can. Kent and Sylvia are more than happy to have you."

"I might," he says. "But Nicole and I are making good progress on the storage rooms. She's going to be here the whole week."

"I think she might need a break," I tell him.

"She'll be here the whole week," he says again, emphasizing each word.

"All right. Well, that's good. I don't want you to be alone if you don't want to be."

"What's the case?" he asks.

I give him a brief overview of what's been happening today.

"That's a lot," he says. "The woman in the attic… Could she have been running from someone? Think of every scary movie ever made. Someone trying to escape always runs upstairs despite there being a perfectly good means of egress."

"I thought about that," I say. "It's the only thing that makes sense. I just need to find who she was running from."

We talk a little more about the case, then he updates me on Cupcake's newest project and other discoveries they made in the storage room. I wish I had been there for some of them, but I know there will be plenty more when I am around. I go to bed exhausted but also hoping morning comes quickly.

CHAPTER SIXTEEN

I ARRIVE AT THE DEPARTMENT EARLY THE NEXT MORNING CARRYING coffee and donuts from a little place down the street. Cartwright hasn't gotten in yet when I walk in, so I head straight for the war room. There are notepads on the table, so I start writing out the statements I got from the neighbors, recording the sparse details so we can go back through them later.

"You took getting started early seriously," Detective Cartwright says when he comes in a few minutes later.

"I brought coffee," I tell him, gesturing at the cup still left in the carrier on the table. "I figured we deserve something better than the stuff here. No offense to the hardworking coffeemaker of the Briar Glen Police Department."

"It's not great," he says. "And if the coffeemaker is offended by that, it should get itself together and work harder."

"Agreed," I say. "There are also donuts."

"Now you're really speaking my language," he says.

I look up at him. "Because you're a police officer?"

"I'm sure there's some sort of '-ist' I could call you right now because of that," he says. "But I'm too tired to think about it right now, so, yes, because I'm a police officer. And an inner fat ass with a sweet tooth that never shuts up."

"I respect that," I say, reaching into the box for a second donut of my own and then sliding the rest toward him.

I bite down into the cinnamon-and-sugar-coated ring and immediately think of Emma. I could have gone for a batch of her cinnamon rolls this morning. I think of the ones that are waiting in the freezer at the Harlan house and tell myself I'll make them as soon as this is over and I'm back home.

"What are you doing?" he asks.

"Getting some statements written out so that they can go into the records," I say. "I heard something really interesting last night that I wanted to tell you about. I don't know for sure that it means anything, but if it does, it could be important. Sylvia was telling me that a couple of months ago she heard a story from one of her friends that a woman went missing after being picked up by an ambulance. I do realize that I just told you that I heard from somebody who heard from somebody, but I can't ignore something about a strange ambulance being related to people going missing."

"Let's see what we can find," the detective says. "Did she have any other information other than that? Who it was or where it happened?"

"She didn't tell me who it was. I don't think that the woman who told her the story told her. But she did mention that she was pretty sure she heard about a woman going missing right around that same time she saw it on the news, so it was probably local."

"That helps," he says.

We take to digging and creative searching, but finally, Mason shows me a case from a few months ago.

"Carla Perkins," he says, reading through the file. "Still classified as a missing person. According to this, a neighbor heard a loud sound, and when they looked out, they saw a stretcher being loaded into an ambulance that rushed away. She never arrived at the hospital and was reported missing soon after. Her roommate wasn't home at the time but was notified that two of the window alarms went off and when the alarm company called to check, no one responded. In keeping with policy, they sent the police. They found the front door unlocked, and so they went inside.

"They found some blood and a bullet hole. The theory is that the sound of the gunshot set off the window alarms. The alarm company confirmed this could happen and that if there was gunfire in the house, it very well could have triggered the alarms on the windows. They were based on the windows' movement, and the sound of the shot could cause enough movement to trigger the alert. They were never able to find out where the ambulance came from or where it took her. The timing of each step of what happened was obviously really suspicious."

"Yeah," I say. "You said that the neighbor heard a loud sound and then looked out to see the woman being loaded into the ambulance. If it was a gunshot that they heard, why would the ambulance already be there when they looked out?"

"Exactly," Mason says. "The neighbor's statement was that they saw two EMTs putting the stretcher into the ambulance, then they got in and drove away. They had no reason to think that there was anything suspicious about the ambulance. It had lights and everything, so they felt like it was authentic."

"Just like the one in front of the McCain house. Only when you look at it more closely, you realize that it doesn't fit in with any of the services," I say. "And Sylvia says there were two EMTs there, too."

My thoughts about the EMTs are shifting rapidly. I started this investigation worrying about them and what might have happened to them that made them disappear. Now I'm wondering if they could have done this. But who were they? And why did they go after Erin and Sophie?

"We need to find out really what was going on that night," Mason says. "I want to go through Erin's and Sophie's phones and find out if either of them might have called for help. Or called anyone else."

"I don't think either of them called that ambulance," I say. "I don't know how it got there, but I don't think the people in it were sitting around listening to emergency reports and responded to a call."

"I don't either," he says. "But we have to find out."

"We should call Ron and ask if he can give us access to Erin's phone," I say. "That will be a lot faster than trying to get the records from the phone company. We should do that too, just in case something was deleted, but I'd like to get a look at her call log and any texts as soon as possible."

"I'll give him a call," the detective says.

Ron answers immediately, and Detective Cartwright explains that we need to see Erin's phone. The call lasts only a few seconds, and when Mason finishes, he tells me that Ron agreed to hand the phone over without any hesitation. I appreciate his willingness to cooperate, but

I'm still interested in getting the full records from the phone company so that we can make sure nothing was removed from the phone before we get it.

Detective Cartwright had caught Ron just before he left the house to go to the hospital and asked him to bring the phone along with him. We go to the hospital and meet up with him to get the phone.

"Do you have the access code?" I ask when he hands over the phone.

He leans over and runs his finger along the dots on the screen to create a pattern. It unlocks the phone, and I repeat the pattern in my head a few times to commit it to memory so I can open the phone again later if I need to.

"Are there any updates about Erin's condition?" I ask.

Ron shakes his head. "The doctor says that she's responding to treatment, but that's what she's been saying this whole time, so I'm not sure what to think. Dr. Bishop is supposed to be back soon, and I'm hoping he'll tell me more since he's the primary doctor on the case."

"Thanks for this," Mason says, indicating the phone. "We'll get it back to you as soon as possible." He pauses. "Did you look at it or erase anything from it?"

"No," Ron says. "I just brought it from the house."

"All right, thank you."

Ron heads back for the elevator to return to Erin's room, and Mason opens the phone again. He goes to the recent calls and sees that there was one from late the night before the incident happened.

"Sophie," I say, pointing out the name. "She did call her. Ron said that Erin frequently couldn't sleep and would stay up late watching TV. There were snacks in the kitchen, and it looked like a lot more than she would prepare just for herself. It looks like Sophie called her and then came over to hang out. Her car was in the shop, so she had to have used a rideshare company to get there, unless Erin went and picked her up."

"Which is entirely possible," Mason says. "They didn't live that far apart. Maybe she called because something was bothering her and she wanted to talk. Erin told her that she was alone and couldn't sleep, so she should just come over and stay the night. She went and picked her up, or she got a ride, and they were both there when the attack happened."

"But why was Erin insisting that the EMT was helping her?" I ask. "If those people are the ones responsible for this attack, why would she be so worried about the man she said was helping her? That just doesn't make sense."

"She was badly hurt. She had a head injury. She could have just misinterpreted what was going on."

"But she didn't ask about Sophie," I say. "She hasn't said anything about her. She has only asked about the EMT. I think that all but eliminates the possibility that she gave her a ride to the house. Sophie might have arrived as the attack was happening and run to hide. Erin might not have ever realized she was even there."

"We need to get Sophie's phone," he says.

Almost as if on cue, his phone rings in his pocket. He answers it, and he meets my eyes, lifting his eyebrows slightly as if to signal there's something significant about the call.

"We'll be right there," he says. He ends the call. "That was the medical examiner's office. He finished the examination of Sophie's body."

"Let's go," I say.

We arrive at the medical examiner's office and are immediately ushered back to his private office. Mason and I sit across the desk from Dr. Jarod Perry, ready to find out what he knows about Sophie Berman and her strange death in the McCain attic.

"Thank you for coming to speak with me," he says.

"Absolutely. We appreciate any information you can give us," Detective Cartwright says.

"I have to tell you, this is a very strange circumstance, but to me, it looks like an accidental death. It appeared to me that she fell and accidentally impaled her thigh on the fire poker. It cut her femoral artery, and she bled out. The death would have taken only a matter of minutes, and she would have been unconscious and far less than that," he says.

"You believe this was an accident?" I ask.

"From the angle that the poker went into her leg and the depth of the cut, yes. I can't be completely positive of all the circumstances, of course, but it seems like she was moving fairly quickly, the poker was lying on the floor with the point protruding, and when she fell, it was just a horrific freak accident that she hit it and it punctured her leg."

"Did you find anything with her body?" Mason asks. "Her phone or anything?"

"I didn't find a phone, but I did find this." He picks a small envelope up from the desk and hands it to the detective. "It was in her pocket."

Mason tips the envelope over, and a key slides out into his palm. He looks at it from different angles, then hands it to me.

"That's it?" he asks.

"Her wallet with her ID and some cash," Dr. Perry says. "But that's it. No jewelry, phone, anything else."

We leave the medical examiner's office in silence. I'm lost in my thoughts, trying to make sense of what we just learned. I thought there would be more to what he found, but now there's almost the same dead-end disappointment that came with leaving the closed hospital. It hasn't prodded us any further. If anything, it just confirms to me that Sophie was hiding in the attic during the attack.

"I'm going to bring you back to the department, and I want you to go talk to Carson Berman," Mason says. "The two of you seem to get along well. I'm going to keep digging into the ambulance and see what I can turn up."

"I was thinking the same thing," I tell him.

CHAPTER SEVENTEEN

I GO TO THE HOSPITAL LOOKING FOR CARSON AND FIND OUT THAT he is not in today. They give me his contact information, and I call him.

"Carson, this is Dean Steele," I say when he answers.

"Hey, Dean," he says. "What can I do for you?"

"I actually need to talk to you again. Could we meet up someplace?" I ask.

"Sure. I'm just out running a couple of errands right now, getting some things taken care of, but I can stop. Where are you now?"

"I'm actually at the hospital," I say. "I thought you might be here, so I came looking for you."

"Oh. No, I decided I need some time to myself after what happened with Sophie," he says. "I'm taking a few days off."

"That's a good idea," I tell him.

"There's a coffee shop not too far from the hospital. Thompson's. I can meet you there in a few minutes," he says.

"That sounds perfect. I'll see you then."

I consider going to check on Erin again but decide they will get in touch with me when there's a change. I don't want to push too much and risk Ron no longer being cooperative with the investigation. The coffee shop is easy to find, and I order an iced brew, wanting the caffeine but not needing the extra heat on the steamy summer day. Carson comes in a few minutes later and joins me perched at the counter in front of the window.

"Are you going to get a drink?" I ask.

He looks over at the menu and makes a contemplating sound. "Yeah, I think I will. I'll be right back."

He returns a few moments later with what looks like iced tea and sits down on another of the high barstools.

"Are you all right talking about your sister here?" I ask.

I don't want him to be uncomfortable having the conversation in public or feel like he's going to get too emotional. He takes a sip of his drink and looks down into the cup for a second before meeting my eyes again.

"Yeah, I can do it," he says.

"All right. Detective Cartwright and I went to the medical examiner's office today and spoke to him about Sophie. His ruling is that her cause of death was accidental. She was in the attic at the McCain house and fell on a fire poker," I tell him gently but clearly. He strikes me as a person who would rather be told things straight out than have someone attempt to preserve his feelings. "The poker punctured her femoral artery, and she bled out."

He draws in a shuddering breath and sets his drink down, putting his hand over his mouth and rubbing it back and forth as he stares at the counter.

"You're saying she wasn't murdered?" he asks.

"Not according to the medical examiner's findings," I say. "He is confident it was an accident."

He sighs, his eyes returning to the same spot on the counter like he can see Sophie there. After a few seconds, he looks at me.

"I just don't know what I'm supposed to feel right now," he says.

"I know," I tell him. "And I completely understand that. No one expects you to feel any certain way or to even know what you're supposed to do right now. I'm so sorry you're going through this. But I do need to ask you about a couple more things."

He nods. "All right."

"Thanks." I reach into my pocket for the key that Dr. Perry gave us. "The medical examiner found this on Sophie's body. Do you have any idea what it might be to?"

Carson takes the key from me and flips it back and forth as he examines it. He eventually shakes his head and hands it back to me.

"I have no idea. It doesn't look like the key to her apartment. She usually used the keypad on the door, anyway. I only have a real key because the battery has gone out in the keypad before, and she wants me to be able to get in and out if that happens again." He pauses and seems to think over what he just said. "I guess not anymore."

"He said the key and her wallet were the only things he found on her body. He didn't even find her phone. Does that seem odd to you?" I ask.

He gives a teary laugh and shakes his head. "No. Sophie was notorious for forgetting her phone. She would lose it all the time. I can't even tell you how many times I've had to call her over and over just to help her find it, or she'll get to my place and have just left it at home."

"The phone wasn't found in the attic or at the McCain house either. Do you think it's probably at her apartment?" I ask. "I didn't notice it when we were looking through her place, but I didn't really search that deeply either."

"It probably is," he says. "I'm sure I can find it for you. I should probably start cleaning out her apartment, anyway."

"I could come with you," I offer.

He nods, and we leave the coffee shop to head for Sophie's apartment. He lets us in the same way he did the first time we came to the apartment, and I glance around, not expecting anything to be different but looking, anyway.

"It's probably going to be somewhere like tucked into the bed or in the bathroom," he tells me. "That's the kind of thing she did."

We walk around the apartment, and he comes out of her bathroom holding the phone. "Here it is. It was sitting on the counter. She was probably getting ready to go over to Erin's and just left it sitting there."

He looks at the phone with tears in his eyes and then hands it over to me. I touch the screen and it lights up, but it asks for a passcode.

"Do you know the passcode to access the phone?" I ask.

He cringes slightly. "No, I'm sorry. She never gave me the code."

"That's all right. I'll just have to request access to the records from the phone company. I already know that she called Erin late the night before all this happened. I know you said that she wasn't dating or going through a breakup or anything, but can you think of any reason why she would be up in the middle of the night and going over to the McCain house?" I ask.

"Sophie was always a night owl. It was just the type of person she was. She had to force herself to be up and doing things during the day like a normal person. Even though she would try, sometimes she just couldn't get to sleep at night. I'm not sure why she would call Erin. Maybe there was something going on at the hospital that she didn't tell me about," he says. "Or she could have known that Erin was alone too, and so she thought they could keep each other company."

"That makes sense," I say.

"I don't understand what's going on," Carson says. "What happened to my sister? I know you say she wasn't murdered, but what happened to her? Why was she even in the attic to begin with? How would she have found that door? Why did someone go after them at all? And where are the EMTs who were supposedly there? I just don't understand how all of this could have happened and no one saw or heard anything."

"We're trying to get answers to all those questions," I reassure him. "I know this is a lot, and you're going through something unimaginable right now, but I'm asking you to trust me. I didn't take on this investigation for no reason. I want to know what happened and why. And I'm going to do absolutely everything in my power to get those answers."

"Here's another one," Mason says, pointing to the screen where he's pulled up a news article. "It says an ambulance was seen near the scene of a minor accident off Hayden Road. When people drove past, they saw the ambulance and another car that had just pulled up behind the accident. The people in that car were interviewed and said that they saw what looked like an EMT near the car when they were approaching. But then as they pulled over, the EMT waved, got into the ambulance, and drove off. They said that the people inside the car were disoriented and not sure what happened, but they were fine. They said the EMT was trying to help them out of the car so they could get medical care. They called for another ambulance and were told that they hadn't gotten any other calls about the accident. No one knew anything about that ambulance, and the people in the car insisted that it was their guardian angels."

"That's not the first time we've heard that phrase," I say. "It seems like a strange ambulance or unidentified EMTs appearing at accidents or roadside emergencies should seem odd, but everyone reporting it is acting like it was a miracle that these people were there. Even though they drove off without providing any true medical care or calling in a real emergency team."

"But they were there without anyone calling," Mason points out. "That's the thing that's consistent across all the stories."

"These EMTs are showing up in places where people need help but then leaving when anyone else shows up or notices them," I say. "But that doesn't fit with what happened at Erin McCain's house. She wasn't in any kind of distress or having any kind of emergency that she reported or that anyone would have known about. She was inside her house."

"What about the blood on the floor and the counter?" he asks.

"Even if that happened while she was alone in the house, she didn't call for help. How would anyone know that she needed the assistance?" I ask.

"What are you thinking then?" he asks.

"I think she was targeted. They didn't show up there by happenstance or because she got hurt. I don't think we're going to see any call for emergency assistance from Sophie's phone records, either. I think they knew exactly what they were doing when they went after her. Just like the woman who disappeared in the mysterious ambulance. She was picked up but never made it to a hospital, and the timing of the sound of the gunshot and her being loaded into the ambulance only makes sense if they were already there when the gunshot happened. It was too fast."

There's a knock at the door, and before either of us can say anything, it flies open. An officer I recognize as one of those doing some digging in the investigation, Officer Bask, bursts in.

"Dispatch just got a call," he says. "There's a fire. It's at Melissa Garrison's house."

CHAPTER EIGHTEEN

Detective Cartwright and I look at each other and immediately jump to our feet.

"When did the call come in?" he asks.

"Just a few minutes ago. Some of the guys were talking about it, and I recognized the address."

"Thanks, Hank," Mason says, grabbing the keys and wallet he set on the table.

He rushes out of the room without saying anything to me, but he doesn't need to. I follow right behind, and we run across the parking lot to where his car is waiting. We jump inside and are already rolling before either of us is buckled in.

Billowing black smoke is visible over the trees as we're approaching the neighborhood, which is only a few minutes' drive away from Erin and Ron McCain's house. The road has been blocked off by the fire trucks and ambulance, and there are already two police cars at the location. Another sits nearly perpendicular across the road to stop anyone from getting too close to the house. We stop close to that car and hop out. The officer standing by his car takes a defensive step forward, then recognizes Mason.

"Detective Cartwright," he says.

"What's going on here?" he asks.

"House fire," he says. "No cause as of right now. Still getting the blaze under control."

"Let us through," he says.

The officer steps to the side as if to symbolically allow us to go around his car to where the main action is happening.

The fire trucks have their massive hoses out and are working to soak the house and ensure the flames are fully gone. We rush up to one of the firefighters standing by.

"Was there anyone inside?" I ask, almost frantically. "Did you find anyone inside?"

"Yes," he says. "There appears to be a set of human remains in the living area. We have men bringing it them out."

The detective and I step back and wait until we see two firefighters carrying a body between them. From the distance, I can tell it's a woman. I know it's Melissa Garrison. They put the body on a gurney near the waiting ambulance, and Mason and I rush over. EMTs get in our way, holding out their hands to stop us.

"You don't want to see this," one of them says. "It's pretty gruesome."

"I'm a detective," Mason says.

"And I'm a private investigator," I tell him.

"She's very badly burned," the paramedic says. "And it looks like she was shot in the head. She's also missing a hand."

"Move," Detective Cartwright says.

We go past the paramedics and up to the stretcher. The woman's body is in horrific condition, and I can see the wound where it does appear that she was shot through the forehead. But my focus falls on her wrist. The stump where her hand used to be looks fairly cleanly cut, like it was very purposely amputated by someone who knew exactly what they were doing.

"No sign of the hand?" the detective asks.

"No," the paramedic says. "We looked in the area where the body was found, but we didn't see it or a weapon capable of doing that."

I look around and notice that several neighbors have come out of their houses and are gathering on the sidewalk across the street, watching the action despite being told by the officers to back up and return to their homes. I jog across the street and meet eyes with a man gripping his mail firmly in his hand as if he had just come out here to retrieve it and noticed everything going on.

"Excuse me," I say. "My name is Dean Steele. I'm a private investigator. Can I ask you a couple of questions?"

"I don't know anything about what's going on," he says immediately. "I just heard a commotion and came out here to see all this."

"You didn't notice the fire?" I ask.

"I was all the way downstairs in my office. It's in the basement. I can't see or hear much of anything from in there. I always come out here and get my mail around this time every day, and I saw all this going on when I came upstairs, so I thought I'd come see what was happening," he says.

"And all the emergency workers were already here?" I ask.

"Yes," he says.

"All right, thank you."

I move down the line to a woman wearing the kind of housedress I've seen in pictures of my grandmother that Emma showed me.

"Ma'am, can you tell me what you saw here? Did you notice anything before the emergency responders showed up?"

"I saw the fire," she says. "I was cleaning the house, and I noticed some smoke through the upstairs window. I looked out, and the house was on fire. I called 911, but they said they'd already gotten the report and were on their way."

"Did you see anything else?" I ask. "Anyone around the house or anything strange that stood out to you?"

"No," she says. "I was just so frightened of the fire that I went downstairs and got my fire extinguisher just in case the firefighters didn't get here on time."

It sounds almost absurd, but by the tears in her eyes, I know she's telling the truth. I can imagine her standing in her living room, watching the fire through her window and clutching the fire extinguisher in case she needed to defend her own home.

"Do you know the woman who lives in that house?" I ask.

"Melissa," she says. "I don't know her very well. She was young and didn't come over for tea or anything. But we've chatted a few times. Seems like a nice girl." Her hand goes to her chest. "Is that her they carried out? Oh lord, is she dead?"

"Yes," I tell her, knowing that no notifications have been made, so I technically shouldn't be sharing that information, but she was going to figure it out. I might as well be honest with her. "That's why it's extremely important that we find out what happened here. We need to know how that fire started."

"I don't know," she says. "I didn't see anything strange. Wait, I did see a car drive by earlier. Something small, beige. I'm sorry I can't think of anything else. I didn't really pay attention to it except for noticing that it drove by a couple of times. But it didn't stop anywhere that I saw."

"Thank you. That's very helpful."

"Did someone do this to her?" she asks, sounding on the edge of panic. "Do I need to be afraid?"

"Ma'am, there is no need for you to think that you are in danger. We're just investigating this incident," I tell her.

The neighbors have noticed that I'm talking to people and are moving away from me, not wanting to get involved. I'm able to stop a couple, but they give me the same information as the first two. They didn't see or hear anything until they saw the smoke. I ask them about the nondescript vehicle the woman saw driving down the street multiple times, and neither of them knows what she's talking about.

"What did you get?" Mason asks when I head back over to him.

"Not much," I say. "None of them saw anybody around the house or anything strange. The only thing is that one of the women thinks she saw a small, beige car drive up and down the road a few times, but it didn't stop anywhere near the house."

"A small, beige car?" Mason asks. "Like every third person owns?"

"I told you, not much," I say. "Clearly, someone was here. She didn't shoot herself in the middle of the forehead and cut off her own hand. But no one saw anybody."

"Or they saw someone and aren't processing it because they've seen them so many times before," Cartwright says. "We need to find out where Ron McCain has been all day. This fire could have been set with a delayed device. We have no idea how long ago it was actually started. I want to know everything that he's done today," he says.

"You think Ron McCain murdered Melissa Garrison?" I ask.

"His mistress who his wife is now going to find out about because he was with her when his wife was brutally attacked? Yeah, I think it's possible," he says.

"Why would he cut off her hand?" I ask. "And where is it?"

"I don't know. But I still need answers from McCain. We need to find him. Now."

It doesn't take long for us to find Ron McCain. He's exactly where I was expecting him to be. At the hospital with Erin. Rather than going to the hospital to have this extremely sensitive conversation with him, Detective Cartwright calls him and asks that he come to the station so that we can ask him a few questions.

"We need to find Melissa Garrison's next of kin as quickly as possible. They need to be notified of her death pronto. We're going to have to tell Ron about it, and I don't want the news spreading around and getting to her family before we can," he says. "Hollings is officially handling the fire. I'm sure he's on it, but I hope he works fast."

Ron appears at the station not too long later, looking bewildered and tired. I look him over for any signs of a struggle or any other indication he might have been involved. This situation is making him seem extremely suspicious, but I can't fully bring myself to believe that he is the one who did this to Melissa. Not only would he know that it would be extremely obvious right off the bat that he would have motive, but he was at the hospital nearly all day. I highly doubt that this was some kind of spur-of-the-moment crime that just sprang out of him. If it were, he wouldn't be calm and steady of mind enough to be able to cover it up so easily.

"What's happening?" he asks when he sees us. "Why didn't you just come to the hospital? I should be there with Erin. The doctors were working on bringing her out of her sedation, and I want to be there when she wakes up."

"This isn't a conversation we could have at the hospital," Mason says. "Please come with me."

We go into a conference room and close the door. It's more comfortable than an interrogation room and isn't being monitored by other officers. It should put Ron at more ease, but I know that Detective Cartwright is ready to transfer right over to an official questioning room if he gets even a hint that Ron could have had anything to do with the murder or the fire.

"Can I get you something to drink?" I ask Ron.

"Water," he says.

"Mason?" I ask.

"Water would be good," he says. "We'll wait for you."

I go to the break room and get three glasses of water, then go back to the heavy tension of the conference room. Ron is staring at the detective, waiting for him to say something, and Mason is staring back, the suspicion obvious in his eyes. I hand each of them water and sit down so I'm positioned between them.

"I need you to go through all of your movements today," Mason says flatly. "Everything you did."

"I was at the hospital with Erin," he says. "Just like I've been since I got here, except for when I went home to sleep."

"I want to know everything you did. From the time you woke up until you got the call from me," the detective says more firmly. "I know you were at your house this morning."

Ron nods. "I woke up early. I had breakfast. Then I left for the hospital. I even brought some of Erin's favorite pastries with me, just in case she might be awake and would be able to eat them. I sat with her until around noon, and then I left to get some lunch and make a couple of calls for work."

"Where did you get lunch? The hospital cafeteria?" Mason asks.

"No, I went to Thompson's. They have good coffee and sandwiches and stuff. The nurses said it would be good for me to take a break and see something other than the hospital for a little while. Why?" His eyes flash back and forth between us. "What's going on? What happened?"

"Do you have a receipt from when you went to lunch?" I ask.

"Yes, and the notification on my phone from when I paid," he says.

"And after that, you said you made some phone calls. Where did you make those calls?" Mason asks.

"I went back to the hospital and went to the meditation garden that you and I talked in, Dean. It's quiet there, and I like it. I also wanted to be close to the hospital in case the doctors called me. I made three phone calls, and then I went back up to Erin's room. I can give you the contact information for the people I talked to," he says.

"That would be good," Mason says.

"I really need to know what's going on," Ron says. "Why are you asking me all these things?"

Mason looks at me. I know he's passing off the responsibility of giving the notification. He's already been pretty hard on Ron, and it would be easier to hear from me. That doesn't mean I'm any more looking forward to saying it.

I move slightly forward so I'm leaning toward Ron, hoping that gives him a sense of security and comfort as I give him the news.

"Ron, we were just called out to a house fire at Melissa Garrison's address," I say.

He's already leaning back away from me, shaking his head almost frantically before I can finish what I have to say.

"Human remains were found inside. We believe it was Melissa."

"No...," he says. "No... that can't be true."

"I'm sorry," I tell him. "I know this is a lot to process, especially after everything you've already gone through. But you have to understand why we needed to find out your movements and know what you were doing today. This doesn't look good for you."

"For me? I didn't do anything to Melissa. I would have no reason to hurt her. We just talked last night. We called off the arrangement between us," he says.

"The arrangement between you?" Detective Cartwright asks, sounding slightly incredulous that he's even saying those words.

"Yes. We didn't think of it as a relationship. Not a real one, anyway. It was just an arrangement, and we agreed it isn't good for us to even consider continuing, and I need to be fully focused on Erin right now. It was a mutual decision that both of us were perfectly fine with. Like I told you, Dean, we were very clear with each other from the beginning. We weren't in love with each other. This wasn't about romance and emotional connection. We were friends and enjoyed spending time together. Yes, we were physical. Yes, I cheated on my wife with her. But there was never anything between us that would make me want to kill her," he says. "I didn't have anything to do with hurting either one of them."

The words linger in a dense silence around us.

This man has had both his wife and his mistress horrifically attacked in a matter of a few days. Is it possible that this has something to do with him? What could he have possibly done that would trigger this kind of brutal violence—but not to him?

Them

Mistakes can be fixed. That's what they had to remind themselves. Things could go wrong, but they could be remedied. It just takes some creativity. Some thought. And willingness.

They were willing. They would do anything that needed to be done to fix what happened and continue on the right path. They'd already begun, but there was much more to do.

The police and that private investigator were starting to get in the way. But they weren't going to let it stop them. This was their time. The mistakes had been made. Now it was time to fix them.

CHAPTER NINETEEN

M Y PHONE RINGS, AND I STEP OUT OF THE ROOM TO ANSWER IT.
"Mr. Steele, this is Dr. Bishop," the doctor says when I answer. "I just wanted to let you know that we've gotten Mrs. McCain out of sedation, and she says that she is ready to speak with you."

"She is?" I ask. "Have you told her everything that happened?"

"No," he says. "We told her that there are people trying to find out what happened to her and that they want to talk with her about it. She said she is willing to help as much as she possibly can."

"That's fantastic. Thanks for letting me know," I say. "I'll be over there shortly."

I go back into the room and tell Mason and Ron about the call I just got. Ron jumps to his feet.

"Erin is awake? I need to go be with her. I told her I was going to be there, and I'm not there. She needs me," he says.

"Ron, I understand that you want to be with your wife, but this is an important part of the investigation, and we're going to need you to wait," Mason says. "You can go back to the hospital, but you can't be in the room while we are talking to your wife. She needs to be able to communicate openly, and information could be shared that we don't want to be accessed by the public yet."

"I'm not the public," he says. "I'm her husband."

"We understand that," I say. "But in an investigation like this, there are certain pieces of information that need to be kept confidential to protect the integrity of the entire investigation. There may be details that she remembers that we don't want anyone else to know. And there is still the simple fact that she might not feel as willing to talk if you're there with her. We just need for you to wait while we speak with her, and then you can see her."

Ron isn't easy to convince, but he finally agrees to go back to the hospital and wait in the waiting room while we speak with Erin. He gives me a long, intense look as I walk out of the room, and I carry it with me as the doctor leads us to Erin's room and knocks on the door.

"Come in," she says.

We walk into the room, and I see her fully awake for the first time since I met her. She still looks swollen and bruised, but she's sitting propped up by the bed and makes eye contact with me easily. A slight smile comes to her lips.

"Dean," she says. "What are you doing here?"

"I'm a private investigator," I tell her. "I'm helping Detective Cartwright investigate what happened to you."

I gesture at the detective, who steps up closer to the bed.

"How are you feeling?"

"That's a really hard question to answer," she says with a slight chuckle. "I'm in pain, and I'm really confused. But I think I feel better than I did."

"Fair enough," he says.

Erin looks around us and then at me again. "Where's Ron? Did he come back from his trip?"

With as much as Ron has talked about telling her that he would be there when she woke up, it's hard to remind myself that she was unconscious the entire time and didn't actually know that he had come back and was there with her.

"Yes," I tell her. "We called him yesterday morning after this all happened, and he came right back. He's been here with you the whole time, except at night. Right now, he's out in the waiting room so that we can talk to you a little bit. I know you want to see him, but it would be better for us if you could talk to just us."

THE WOMAN IN THE ATTIC

I look over at the doctor, who catches what I said and pats Erin on the arm.

"I'm going to step out. I'll be back in a while to check on you. If you need anything, use your call button."

"I will," she says. "Thank you."

"I wanted to note that Erin is experiencing some significant issues with her memory. From what she's communicated with us so far, her memory of what happened, and even the time before and after, are very fractured. This is expected with not just the injuries she sustained but also the drugs that were found in her system," Dr. Bishop says.

"Is there anything that can help that?" Detective Cartwright asks.

"Not really," the doctor says. "All we can do is work with what we are able to get from Erin now and hope that more comes to the surface. If you need anything else, I'll be around."

"Thank you," I say.

The doctor closes the door behind him, and we walk up to the side of the bed.

"Thank you for being willing to talk to us," I say.

"I want to know what happened to me," she says. "I want to be able to thank the EMT who tried to help me."

Detective Cartwright and I exchange a glance.

"We're going to talk about that in a moment, but there's something that we need to talk about first," Mason says.

Erin looks nervous. "All right."

"We found Sophie Berman in the attic of your house yesterday morning before we found you in the woods," he tells her. "She's dead."

A hand flies up to cover Erin's mouth as she gasps in horror. Her eyes pool with tears, and she looks back and forth between us like one of us is going to be able to tell her something different.

"She's dead?" she asks in a powdery voice. "What happened to her?"

"Right now, we need information from you," Mason says. "I know this is coming as a serious shock, and we'll make sure you get the details later, but we really need to find out as much from you as we possibly can."

"Erin," I say, stepping up closer to the side of the bed and resting my hands on the edge. "We know that Sophie called you late that night. What happened after that? What do you remember about her being at your house?"

"I don't remember her being there," she says. "She did call me. It was really late, but I was awake. I never sleep very well when Ron is away on business. She said that she was upset about something and really needed a friend, so I suggested that she come over and we could hang out. She said it would be like an old-fashioned slumber party. That's why I was getting all the snacks and stuff together. We were just going to watch TV and eat and talk.

"I knew about when she was going to show up, so I unlocked the front door so she could let herself in. Then I went back into the kitchen to keep putting together the snacks and everything. I don't remember her coming in or seeing her. I do remember hearing the door open. But that's it. The next thing I remember is coming to on the kitchen floor with an EMT saying he was going to help me."

"Can you describe the EMT?" I ask.

"No," she says. "He was wearing a hat and a mask. I don't remember anything else. Then I must have passed out again because the next time I remember anything, I was outside. I was in a lot of pain and was trying to get home, but I didn't really know where to go. I don't know what happened in between. Have you talked to the EMT?"

"We haven't been able to locate the EMT," I tell her.

"You haven't been able to locate him?" she asks, sounding confused and afraid. "That means something horrible happened to him, too. Do you think Sophie could have shown up while I was being attacked, called 911, then we were all attacked again? You said Sophie was in the attic. She could have run there to try to protect herself."

It's the same kind of thought I'd had about her being in the attic, but it doesn't sit right with me anymore. I am convinced the EMTs, or at least the people posing as EMTs, aren't victims in this situation but the ones who are responsible for Erin's attack and Sophie's death. But it leaves me wondering why Erin is so sure that one of them was trying to comfort her when she was going through whatever was happening to her. And what caused her to end up so deep in the woods?

"You're sure that the EMT said he was going to help you?" I ask.

"Yes," she says.

"And you don't remember anything between hearing the door open and coming to with the EMT with you?" Mason asks.

"No," she says. "I told you everything I remember." She wipes tears from her eyes and grabs a tissue from the metal table sitting beside her bed. "I can't believe Sophie's gone. If she hadn't called me, if she hadn't come over to my house..."

"You can't put that on yourself," I say. "You didn't cause this. You didn't do anything wrong, and you can't make yourself feel like that. I appreciate you talking to us. I'm going to get Ron for you."

THE WOMAN IN THE ATTIC

I go out into the waiting room, and Ron pops to his feet from the chair where he'd been sitting with his chin in his hands and his elbows on his knees, his feet bouncing nervously. He comes toward me.

"We're done talking to her for now," I say. "You can go in and see her."

"Did you tell her anything?" he asks.

I know he's asking about Melissa and his affair with her, as well as her gruesome death. I can't imagine the amount of stress and pressure bearing down on this man right now. It's stunning to me that he's even standing. I can't decide if I think it will get worse once he tells Erin and knows her reaction or if he will at least feel some relief that the waiting is over.

"No, I didn't tell her anything," I say. "That's for you to do when the time is right. But Ron, I don't think that you should wait very long. It's going to come out one way or another, and you don't want her to find out from someone else."

He nods and heads for her room. Detective Cartwright's phone rings in his pocket as we're starting down the stairs toward the entrance.

"Cartwright," he says. "All right. Do you know what it's about?" he asks after a pause. "We'll be there." He glances at his watch when he ends the call. "We need to get back to the department."

"What's going on?" I ask.

"That was Mulroney. She said some woman called the station, wanting to speak to whoever was handling the case with the ambulance. She said her son has something he needs to tell us."

CHAPTER TWENTY

"Something he needs to tell us?" I ask.

"Yeah," the detective says. "But she didn't give any more details than that. She wants to speak to us directly. I've got to go meet with the fire marshal about the fire investigation. Since it seems to connect with our case because of the link between Ron McCain and Melissa Garrison, they transferred it over to me. I'm going to have you talk to the kid and his mother. Find out what she's so worked up about and if you think it really has anything to do with the case."

He drops me off, and I go inside to find a woman and a teenage boy already sitting in the few chairs in the reception area. I go up to the desk.

"Are these the people who wanted to talk to Cartwright and me?" I ask.

The officer behind the desk gives a nod. "Yep. Delaney Morris and her son, Tyler."

"I'm going to be talking to them," I say. "I'll bring them on back."

THE WOMAN IN THE ATTIC

She nods and goes back to what she was doing. I walk up to the woman and her son, who looks like he's so nervous about being here he's about to pass out.

"Mrs. Morris, my name is Dean Steele. I'm a private investigator," I say.

"Private investigator?" she asks. "I thought I was going to be able to talk to the detective handling the case."

"I'm helping Detective Cartwright with this investigation. He's busy with another aspect of it right now, and we didn't want you to have to wait, so I'll be talking to you," I say.

She looks slightly hesitant, but then she gives a single nod. "All right."

"You can come on back with me," I say.

"Come on, Tyler," she says, standing up and lightly swatting her son on the upper arm to get his attention.

He looks at me like he had been so wrapped up in his own thoughts he didn't even notice I'd come up to them and then stands up. I bring them into the back and find one of the rooms where witnesses and families are generally brought. It's more comfortable and less intimidating than an interrogation room or a stark conference room.

"Mrs. Morris, can I get you a cup of coffee or something else to drink?" I ask.

"A soda would be great if you have it," she says.

"Sure. Tyler? Can I bring you a drink?"

He keeps his mouth firmly closed and shakes his head. I go to the break room and get three cans of soda and a couple of packets of snacks. Then I bring them back into the room, setting them on the table in front of a large, red couch where the two of them are sitting.

"I thought I'd go ahead and bring something to you anyway," I say to Tyler. "It's hot out there today."

He nods and reaches for one of the sodas. I sit down in the chair positioned across from the couch and take my own drink, sipping it slowly in hopes of creating a calmer atmosphere for the teenager who is clearly on the brink of falling apart.

"So," I say, setting my drink down, "I heard that you called here saying you wanted to talk to the people handling the case with the ambulance."

"Yes," Mrs. Morris says firmly.

"Can you elaborate on that a little?" I ask.

"It was just on the news. A woman was killed, and another one attacked in a house where an ambulance was parked, but no EMTs were found on location and no one knows why it was there," she says.

I knew the information was going to come out at some point, but I wish more had been kept confidential. Even as I'm thinking that though, I realize there's no real way to keep confidential something like a strange ambulance parked in front of a house for hours with a stretcher on the street. Too many people saw it and wanted to talk about it.

"And you say that your son has something he wants to tell us. Does it have to do with this situation?" I ask.

"I think it might. I heard him talking to one of his friends about something that happened, and I think he needs to come clean about it. It could be important." She looks over at her son. "Tyler, go on."

The boy takes a breath, steadying himself as he prepares to tell me whatever information he has.

"My friend Gary and I went out to the old Brower Woods to look around and saw a big, old house that looks like it's right out of a horror movie. We were with a couple of other guys, and no one wanted to go in. Later Gary and I talked about it, and we decided we were going to go inside and see what was there," he says.

"Why?" I ask.

"There are all kinds of stories about that house, and we thought if we could show people in school pictures of the inside and talk about being in there, they would see us differently."

"They wanted to impress the popular kids and get more attention from girls," Mrs. Morris says matter-of-factly.

"I can understand that," I say. "I wasn't exactly what they would call popular when I was in high school. Anyway, so I take it you and Gary went back to the house?"

"Yeah," Tyler says, starting to sound a bit more at ease with me. "We dared each other to go inside and take pictures. It was really dark when we went, and I started getting nervous, but I couldn't go back on what I said. We got back to the house, and I found a piece of the fence that was lifted up, so we went under it. The closest part of the house was the back patio, but the doors were locked, so we broke a window and climbed inside."

"I can't believe my son would do something like this," Mrs. Morris says, closing her eyes and shaking her head. "I thought I raised you better than this."

"I'm sorry, Mom," he says. "I didn't mean to upset you."

"Let's just talk about what happened," I say. "We can deal with the rest of it later. You said you broke a window and went inside."

"Yeah," he says. "It was really dark inside, and it was raining, so we couldn't really see very much. We had our flashlights, and we took some pictures. It wasn't much. Just an old house with some junk in it. But it was seriously creepy inside. We started hearing sounds, and I thought they were animals, but I wanted to get out of there. We decided we were just going to look at a couple more places, take a few more pictures, then we were going to leave.

"We ended up finding the basement, and when we went downstairs, we heard humming, like electricity. In the basement, we found a big metal table and a bunch of chest freezers. You know those big ones that people keep in their garage with extra food? There were like six of those. We couldn't figure out what we just found, and we were going to open one of the freezers, but then the lights turned on."

"The lights turned on?" I ask.

"Yes. We didn't think there was any electricity in the house, but all the lights in the room turned on, and we saw that somebody had come down the stairs. I have no idea who it was. I can't even tell you what they looked like. I was so scared. We pushed them over and ran out of the house. We ran through the front door, and when we got outside, I thought I saw something really weird. Parked in front of the house was what looked like an ambulance."

"An ambulance?" I ask.

"That's what it looked like," he says. "We were running too fast for me to really get a good look at it, but that's what it looked like."

"Do you have any proof?" I ask. "This is a compelling story, but I need to confirm that it actually happened before I can do anything about it."

"We understand," Mrs. Morris says. "Show him, Tyler."

Tyler takes his phone out of his pocket and flips through the screen for a second, then turns it to me. There's an image on the screen, but it's so dark I can't tell what I'm looking at.

"That's the house," he says. "You can keep scrolling through the pictures and see everything we took."

I swipe through the picture gallery, looking at the images of what looks like the inside of an old, abandoned mansion. There's furniture covered in drop cloths and art on the walls. It looks like a couple of the rooms have been largely cleared out while others have been left, much like they were when whoever last lived there either left or died. There are quite a few pictures that show the progression of the two boys through the house, including a few that show the other boy and one that is a reflection of Tyler in a large mirror on the wall. It proves they truly were inside the house and didn't just find these pictures somewhere. But I notice something that bothers me.

"What about the basement?" I ask. "There are no pictures of the freezers or anything."

"We were too scared to take any in the basement," he says.

"Why didn't you come forward sooner?" I ask. "Why didn't you tell anyone what you saw?"

"We were too scared. We thought we'd get in trouble for going into the house."

The boy is obviously shaken up, and though I don't have any proof that what he said he saw in the basement actually existed, I have the tendency to believe him. The ambulance detail is particularly intriguing to me.

I use my phone to pull up a map to find what he called the Bower Woods. Showing it to him, I have Tyler point out where the house is located. I give him a sheet of paper and ask him to draw a map as clearly as he can so that we'd be able to follow it to the old house.

"Thank you for coming in," I say when he's done and I have the finished map in my hands. "I know it wasn't easy. Mrs. Morris, you should be very proud of your son for being so forthcoming with me."

She looks at Tyler, and a softer expression comes over her face. She wraps an arm around his shoulders and gives him a little hug.

"I am proud of him. I'm still furious he would do something like this, but I'm proud of him for telling the truth," she says.

"Good. If you can think of anything else that might be important, give me a call. We might need to talk to you again too," I say.

They leave, and I call Detective Cartwright.

"Are you still in your meeting about the fire?" I ask.

"No, we just finished. Why?" he asks. "Did that meeting with the kid actually come up with something?"

"Possibly," I say. "But it's going to take some investigating to find out."

"I'll be back at the station in just a few minutes, and you can fill me in," he says.

We meet in the investigation room. He brings me a massive sandwich and some fries for lunch, which I eagerly dive into.

"From the diner up the road," he says. "They make good food."

"It's great. Thank you," I say. "All right. So the woman who called, Mrs. Morris, had overheard her son, Tyler, talking to one of his buddies and decided we needed to hear all about it. Turns out there's a big house out in the middle of something called the Bower Woods."

"I know those woods," he says. "They used to be owned by the Bower family, but they died out a long time ago. That house is still there?"

"Apparently. And there are tons of urban legends and myths about it. These guys decided if they went into the house and brought back proof, they could get the attention of some of the popular kids and the girls would like them," I say.

"Leave it to teenage boys to always try anything and everything to get their hands on girls," he says.

"Something like that. Anyway, they went to the house and took a bunch of pictures of the inside. I saw them. It was definitely eerie in there. I can understand why people would make up stories about it. They said they were planning on leaving after looking down in the basement, because every creepy house has a terrifying basement, I guess. They went down there, and that's when things got really strange. Tyler said they saw a big metal table and at least six chest freezers. They heard the humming of electricity, and then the lights turned on. Somebody was down in the basement with them, but he can't describe them. He said they knocked the person down and ran out. That's when they saw an ambulance parked outside the front of the house."

"An ambulance?" Mason asks.

"Yes. Apparently, that's the detail that his mother thought was the most significant and made her want her son to tell us what happened," I say.

"Any pictures of the freezers in the basement or the ambulance?" he asks.

"No. Tyler said they were too scared to take pictures in the basement, and I'm assuming the same went for when they got outside and saw the ambulance," I say.

"Do you believe him?"

"Like I said, I saw the pictures of the inside of the house. One of them was the classic mirror selfie, so they were definitely inside. I don't know why he would lie about something like seeing the freezers or an ambulance outside to the point of his mother making him come and talk to us about it. If it were a hoax, I would think he'd come clean before he had to come here," I say.

"That's true," Mason says. "I can't imagine this was a fun experience for him. You know, this could just be some squatter taking up residence in an old house and keeping roadkill to eat."

"Roadkill he picks up with an ambulance?" I ask, pointing out the fallacy of his theory.

"We're going to have to go out and see that house."

"I already have a map for how to get there," I say.

"Then let's get what we need and go."

CHAPTER TWENTY-ONE

VENTURING INTO UNFAMILIAR WOODS IS NOT SOMETHING I anticipated doing today, and the hot summer air stinging my neck and sending beads of sweat down my face from my temple makes every step feel heavier. But there's a sense of excitement as we get deeper into the woods, following Tyler's map and hoping that he remembered accurately how they got to the house. This could be something. If the teenager was right and they really did see an ambulance sitting outside the house after being chased away from the basement, this could finally be a new lead.

Or it could be the ramblings of a teenager who scared the living hell out of himself by creeping into a supposedly haunted house on, quite literally, a dark and stormy night.

But I'm willing to go through this to find out.

"If he saw the ambulance sitting outside the house, how did it get there?" Mason asks as we make our way down the makeshift path we found. "There's nothing around here that would let a car through."

THE WOMAN IN THE ATTIC

"He said that the way they came brought them up to the back of the property," I say. "That when they went under the fence, they were closest to the back patio. Then the ambulance was parked at the front of the house when they ran out. That would mean it was driven up from the other direction."

"I wish we had gone that direction," he complains. "I'd much rather be driving at this point."

"We've come this far," I say. "We're not going to turn around now so that we can drive up to the house," I say.

He gives me a look but doesn't say anything else. We continue on through the woods, guzzling the water we brought along with us and wishing for the respite of the rain they experienced when they were trudging toward the house. Finally, we see the imposing structure ahead of us.

"There," I tell him. "We found it. There's the fence that they went under to get onto the property."

"Let's follow it around to the front," the detective suggests. "I want to see where they supposedly saw the ambulance."

Trees and vines have grown up through the fence in some places, making it difficult to follow around, but we climb our way along the edge, following the fairly small grounds around the side and then to the front of the house. When we get to the front of the property, we can see a narrow dirt road leading back into the woods. It isn't smooth or well maintained, but it's clear that it has been used fairly recently.

"There's a gate," I say. We approach the gate and notice a chain with a lock wrapped around it. "It isn't rusted. This isn't an old lock."

Detective Cartwright looks down at the dirt path and follows it back a couple of yards.

"Look, there are tread marks." He points down at the ground at his feet. "Right here. This anomaly right here was on the impressions made of the tires. At least, I'm almost positive it's the same thing. We'd have to take up a cast of these and compare them, but I've looked at those impressions a dozen times. It looks just like it."

"That ambulance was here," I say. "There's something in that house related to it, which means whatever those kids found in there could give us the answers to what happened at the McCain house. We need to see the inside of that house."

"We can't just go inside," he tells me. "We have to get a warrant to allow us to go through the chain and search the property. I'll put in for it as soon as we get back to the department."

"I hate the red tape. I want to go in there right now so badly," I say. "It's right there. I just want to hop the fence, find the window Tyler and his buddy broke, and go into that basement. There's something in there. And we can't touch it."

"I'd say I'd turn my back and let you do it, but then anything you'd find would be inadmissible," he says. "There very well could be something important in there, but we can't do anything about it right now. Let's get out of here so we can get that warrant working."

While the detective goes through the process of getting the warrant that will let us actually go into the house in the woods, I go back to Kent and Sylvia's house to take a shower. Once I've washed away the sweat and remnants of the woods, I go down onto the first floor of the house and into the living room. Neither of them is home, so I have it to myself. I drop down onto the couch to savor some of the peaceful quiet and air-conditioning.

I intended to stay here for a little while, possibly even closing my eyes to catch a few minutes of rest, but I notice the McCain house through the front window. Ron's car has just pulled into the driveway, and he gets out. I watch him walk over to the mailbox and look inside, pulling out a handful of mail that he carries with him to the front door. Dragging myself up off the couch, I go to the front door and call out to him.

"Ron!"

He pauses where he's poised to unlock the door and looks over his shoulder toward me. I glance both ways and jog across the street to him, slowing down when I get to the sidewalk so I can walk up to him.

"Hey, Dean," he says.

"Hi. Taking a break from the hospital?" I ask.

"Erin sent me home to take a shower and eat some real food. She thinks I need some time to myself after being there all day," I say.

"She's probably right," I tell him. "Sitting there like that has got to be stressful."

"But she doesn't have a choice. She just has to stay there as long as they want to keep her. At least the doctors say she's doing well, and they might be able to discharge her in the next day or two," he says.

"That would be great. I know you would be glad to have her home," I say.

"I just hope it isn't too traumatizing for her to come back here. Maybe it will trigger some memories of what happened and she won't want to be here anymore," he says.

"Coming back here triggering her memories would be a good thing," I tell him. "We're still trying hard to figure out exactly what happened and who did this to her, so anything she can remember would be beneficial. Speaking of which, I was hoping I could come inside and look around some. It might help me get a better understanding of what Erin told me when we were talking about what happened that night."

"I thought you were inside. You found…"—he pauses and takes a breath—"the body in the attic."

"I was," I tell him. "But I was very focused on looking for Erin and identifying any threats. I wasn't really paying attention to what else was around me, like the layout of the house. Now that I've gotten a statement from her about what was going on when she was likely attacked, I would like to see the house and try to get a better perspective of it. Would that be all right?"

"I guess that would be fine," he says. "Come on in."

He unlocks the door and steps inside. I follow after him, breathing in the smell of an air freshener I didn't notice the first time I was in the house. The air-conditioning was set just a little too cold, giving me almost the feeling of walking into a hotel. There's even a suitcase sitting just inside the door, the zipper open and some of what's inside spilling out.

"Sorry," Ron says, trying to push the suitcase aside with his foot. "I just dropped everything when I got here after going to the hospital. I didn't feel like taking the time to put it away."

"It's fine," I say. "You've been going through a lot. I don't think anyone expects you to be keeping a perfect house on top of dealing with everything else."

"Erin would hate it. She always fusses at me for leaving my stuff on the floor when I get home. She says I should just carry it right to our bedroom. It would save time and energy." He suddenly looks deeply sad. "I wonder if I'm ever going to get to hear her say that to me again. Once I tell her…"

"You haven't told her yet?" I ask.

"No," he says. "I just can't bring myself to. She's lying in that bed and has been through so much. I don't want to put even more on her and maybe make it harder for her to heal. I know I need to tell her soon, and I'm going to. I just need to find the right moment. I was hoping to do it after she got home. Maybe I should just leave my bag there. That way, I'm already packed for when she kicks me out." He tries to laugh like he's making light of the whole thing, but then his face crumbles, and he hangs his head, covering his eyes.

"I'm sorry," I say, trying to think of some way to comfort him.

I can't even begin to imagine everything he's trying to drag his way through right now. Not only does he have this tremendous secret that he's going to have to tell his wife and that could very well threaten his marriage, but he's also coping with the loss of someone close to him. It doesn't matter what he said was the true nature of their relationship or if he never intended to see her again. Having someone you know that well brutally murdered and mutilated is something no one knows how to deal with, and that will scar him into the future.

"I'm just going to go into the kitchen, if that's all right with you," I say.

He nods, and I walk around him into the back of the house where the kitchen takes up nearly the entirety of the floor space along with a breakfast nook. I have to go past the living room to get to it, but the way that the room is laid out, I can't see the front door if I'm standing at the counter. If I go to a very specific place in the kitchen and look around the corner of the doorway, I can see part of it. Otherwise, it is just the living room.

The bowls of snacks have been cleaned up, and there are no traces of the blood left on the counter or the floor. Ron comes into the room behind me and sees me looking where they were.

He nods. "I cleaned it up. The doctor said she hit her head on something. I'm guessing it was the counter," he says.

"That makes sense," I tell him. "Have you been able to clean up the attic?"

It's a sensitive question, but I'm worried about him. It doesn't matter how I feel about some of the things he's done. He is struggling right now, and I feel a tug to try to help him. I've done enough in my life that I try to remind myself I can't really stand in judgment of anyone, especially not at a time like this. It might not always work, but I try.

"No," he says, shaking his head. "I can't even bring myself to go up there. I closed the door and can't even think about looking. I don't know what I'm going to do."

"I'll help you find a cleanup team," I say. "There are people who specialize in that kind of job. We'll get it taken care of."

"Thank you so much, and thank you for being here for Erin."

"Just doing my job," I say.

"I didn't do anything to her. Or to Melissa. I would never do something like that."

"We're going to find out what happened," I tell him.

Again, I wonder if there's any chance that all this might have something to do with him. But that wouldn't explain the other possible incidents.

THE WOMAN IN THE ATTIC

I spend the next twenty minutes arranging a crime scene cleanup crew to come and handle the cleaning of the attic so that Ron doesn't have to do it. The CSU has already cleared the space, so now all that has to be done is clean up the blood. It will take some effort to remove it from the unfinished wood of the attic floor, but they reassure me that they will get it done as well as they possibly can. There might be some traces left even after the cleaning, and I plan to suggest to Ron that he let me come up and paint over any areas that can't be fully rid of the staining so that they don't have to see it every time they go up to their attic.

When that's arranged, I subtly text Kent to find out if it would be all right to invite Ron over for dinner that night so that he wouldn't be alone. The response is immediate that it would be fine.

"Why don't you come over to Kent and Sylvia's house for dinner tonight?" I ask. "Kent is making stir-fry with steak and chicken."

"That sounds good, but I think I'll just stay here and decompress," he says. "I think I'd just like to be alone."

"I don't think being alone for a long time is a great idea for you right now," I tell him. "It would be nice for you to be with people. Get your mind off of everything for just a little bit. Then you can come back and decompress all you want."

He chuckles. "All right."

"Good."

We walk out of the house, and he locks the door behind him, testing the handle before we head down the sidewalk to Kent and Sylvia's house.

CHAPTER TWENTY-TWO

THE WARRANT COMES THROUGH EARLY THE NEXT MORNING. I'M already at the station when Mason comes into the room, this time being the one bearing coffee, and tells me that we've got everything we need to go into the house and search. I brought along a stronger flashlight so I wouldn't have to walk around with just my phone just in case we were going. I add it to a collection of tools and equipment we load into the trunk of the detective's car so we'll be able to access the house and whatever we might find in it.

Now that we've approached the foreboding old mansion from the back, we have a better idea of its orientation in the woods and use the map to figure out how to access the dirt road we saw leading to the front gate. When we're reasonably sure we've got the right way, we pack everything we need and head out.

The road isn't as easy to find as we would have liked it to be, but once we locate it, I know that anyone who knows exactly what they're looking for would be able to pick it out fairly easily. The way is not smooth,

THE WOMAN IN THE ATTIC

and I end up grabbing the handle above my head to hold myself steady as the car bounces and lurches along the unpaved road. There's a point as we get deeper into the woods when it feels like we aren't going to get anywhere, and my head says we should turn back, but my gut says we need to keep pushing. There's something in that house, and we need to find it.

We finally pull up to the gate in front of the house, and Detective Cartwright pauses. We both look through the windshield at the house. It's strangely beautiful in the light, but there's still an ominous energy surrounding it that I don't look forward to immersing myself in for long.

"I'll get the chain off," I offer, climbing out of the car.

I go around to the trunk and take out a heavy bolt cutter. Carrying it over to the gate, I examine the lock on the chain again. There is little evidence of aging, no rust, nothing that would suggest this lock has been secured this way for many years. Probably not even weeks. The bolt cutter severs the chain easily, and I remove it, tossing it over to the side of the road so that I can open the gate. It opens easily, without any of the resistance that would come from disuse. I get back into the car and look at the detective.

"Someone uses this place often," I tell him. "That gate barely even made a sound when I opened it. Whoever it is wants the house to look like it's still abandoned and as creepy as possible so that people won't get near it, but they're using it for something."

"And we're going to find out what," he says.

We drive through the gate and up the cracked drive to park next to the side of the house. As we get out, I listen carefully to my surroundings. Among the sounds of the forest, I can hear a distinct humming. I point up like I'm indicating the sound waves.

"Do you hear that?" I ask.

"Sounds like something mechanical," Mason says.

"A generator," I say. "This place is hooked up to a generator. The boys must not have seen it, and they said it was raining, so they wouldn't have heard it before they went inside."

"But Tyler did say that he heard electricity when he was down in the basement," he says.

"They really did see freezers," I say. "And they could hear them running."

"Let's find out what's so important that's being kept in those freezers," he says.

We walk to the front door and try it. It's locked, which immediately strikes me. Tyler specifically said they got out of the house through the front door. He obviously didn't lock it behind himself, which means someone else did.

"Do you want to break it open or just go around back to where the boys went in?" I ask.

"Let's go around back. It's too hot to be breaking down doors right now," Mason says.

I chuckle, and we walk around the house to the back patio. I can see the doors Tyler described and then the window broken in. I gesture to it.

"After you," I say.

"Afraid of a haunted house, Steele?" he asks.

"As one of my favorite old movies says, 'They're mortar, stone, and wood.' I'm just less a fan of the idea of getting cut on any glass that's left around that window frame," I say.

"Thanks," he says.

He climbs through the window with little difficulty, and I follow. It would definitely be an easier route for the smaller teenagers, but we made it through. The bright daylight outside pours through the windows, delving into the shadowy corners and illuminating the first room so we can look around easily. I recognize it from the pictures that Tyler showed me and use my memory of those pictures to guide me through to the next room. There are heavy curtains pulled over most of the other windows, keeping the other rooms darker than the first, so we rely on our flashlights to guide us through.

I listen for any sounds around us that might come from someone else being there. I don't hear anything. The house feels empty, but that doesn't necessarily mean it is. I've been shocked by particularly stealthy people before. We move through the house, shining our lights throughout the rooms until we get to the door that I had Tyler describe to me after drawing the map.

Detective Cartwright uses the end of his flashlight to knock on the door.

"Briar Glen Police," he announces. "If anyone is down there, have your hands up. We're coming in."

He pauses for another moment, then opens the door. I shine my flashlight up and see a chain hanging from the ceiling. I tug it, and a lightbulb turns on. We exchange a glance and continue down the stairs. Mason announces us again as we take our first steps, but there's no reaction. We only need to go halfway before I see that Tyler was telling the truth.

THE WOMAN IN THE ATTIC

Set on the polished cement floor of the basement is a brushed metal table with a sheet folded at the foot. As I walk further down the steps, I can see several oversized white chest freezers.

"Holy shit," Mason mutters.

"What the hell is this?" I ask.

"What do you think is in those freezers?" he asks.

"I'm not sure, but we have to find out."

I walk up to the first and press the heels of my hands against the edge of the lid. I lift it, and it immediately drops down from my hands again as I stumble back a few steps.

"What?" Mason asks. "What is it?"

Taking a breath, I go back to the freezer and open the lid again. A woman's face stares up at me. It's just her head, nestled among two legs and an arm. Each piece is carefully wrapped in clear plastic and appears to be labeled.

"Remember that 'holy shit'?" I ask.

"Yeah."

"Now would be the time to say it."

He comes over and looks down into the freezer with me.

"Oh, what the fuck," he says.

"We're going to need some backup," I say.

He immediately gets on his phone and calls for backup, explaining that we're going to need officers and the forensic unit.

While he talks, I go to the next freezer. Bracing myself for whatever I'm going to find inside, I open it. This one is empty, but there's a reddish stain at the bottom that tells me it wasn't always this way. The third freezer contains a torso and another head, while the fourth has two more arms and a pair of feet. The fifth freezer is also empty, and the sixth contains only one thing. Something I wasn't expecting to see, but now that I do, I know we're both closer to and much further from the answers we've been searching for.

"What did you find?" Detective Cartwright asks, ending his call and coming over to me.

I gesture down at the single female hand resting on the bottom of the freezer.

"I have a feeling if we run a DNA test on that hand, it will come back to Melissa Garrison," I say.

"But what is it doing here?" he asks.

I shake my head. "I don't know. But this whole place needs to be searched thoroughly."

I look across the room to where a large cabinet stands against the far wall. I walk over to it and begin going through it. It's full of folded sheets and medical implements. A shiver runs through me at the thought of what whoever uses this place does with the scalpels, large knives, and suture materials. In a drawer I find a stack of manila folders.

"Look at this," I say to Detective Cartwright.

"What are they?" he asks.

I flip open one of them and see a woman's face looking up at me from a picture attached to the top of the folder. It's obvious the picture is of a head that has been removed from its body, and I recognize it as the head I saw when I opened the first freezer. There's a single page of notes under the picture, but the only thing on it that I can understand is the number 6 written on the top line.

"It looks like medical records of some kind, but they're written in code. I don't know what they say."

"Is there a name?" he asks.

"No," I tell him, turning the file toward him so he can see the page of notes. "This is all that's on this one. I'm positive this is the head I saw in the first freezer."

I set the folder down and open the next one. Instead of seeing a face, the picture is of an arm. Much like the first file, everything written on the page appears to be in some kind of code, and there is a number on the top: 9.

"What are the numbers?" Mason asks.

"They identify the parts," I say.

I go back over to the first freezer and open it. Looking down at the head, I notice a 6 written on the plastic wrapped around it.

"This is the same head, and it is marked with a 6," I say. "And this arm is marked with a 9. Both of these are of legs that are marked with 3s."

"How many are there?" he asks.

I look through the rest of the files, reading the numbers. "Fourteen. That's the number on the hand."

Overhead, we hear the rest of the officers and the forensic team arrive. The detective goes upstairs to meet them and bring them down into the gore-filled basement. He sets them to work photographing and recording the scene, then collecting the remains so they can be transferred to the medical examiner's office.

"This completely changes everything," I tell him when he comes back over to me. "We're not just looking at Erin McCain and Sophie Berman anymore. The possibility of other sightings isn't just arbitrary.

We're looking at the possibility of far more victims here. The question is, how are we going to identify them?"

CHAPTER TWENTY-THREE

THE FORENSIC UNIT PROCESSES THE GRUESOME SCENE IN THE basement while other officers carefully search the rest of the house, looking for anything else that might be connected. Detective Cartwright calls Dr. Perry to fill him in on what's happening so that he will be prepared for the influx of body parts that will be coming to his office soon.

"He almost sounds like he's looking forward to it," he says when he ends the call.

"Well, I guess that's the way you have to look at it when you're the medical examiner. A big puzzle that needs to be solved," I say.

While the other units continue with their work, we take the records we found and bring them back to the war room in the police department so we can begin the process of connecting the images and details of the body parts to the victims they belong to. Some are going to be far more challenging than others. That's obvious right from the beginning. But we have to do it. We have to find out who these parts belong to and how they ended up in those freezers in the basement of a supposedly abandoned house. There are families out there wondering what happened to their loved ones, and we are getting closer to being able to tell them. We have to work as hard as we can to make that happen.

We put the files in order according to the numbers and look at the first one. There's no picture attached to it, which leaves us with nothing to go on.

"Maybe the picture fell off," I say. "We should call the CSU and have them search the cabinet to see if it's there."

While he does that, I sift through the pseudo medical records to see if I can make any sense of the code used to fill the lines with what look like notes and commentary. Nothing comes to mind, so I turn my attention back to the pictures. It's going to be extremely difficult to try to figure out to whom the dismembered body parts belong, so I pull two files toward me. Each has a picture of a woman's head inside. Not yet wrapped in plastic, they look like they were photographed very soon after being removed from their bodies.

"She looks familiar," I say, pointing to the head marked with the number 6. "I'm sure I've seen her before."

Detective Cartwright stares down at the image for a few seconds before straightening. He sits down in front of his laptop and types something into it before turning it toward me.

"Carla Perkins," he says.

Stunned, I draw the computer closer so I can get a better look at the picture he's showing me.

"Carla Perkins?" I ask. "The woman who was picked up by the ambulance but never brought to a hospital after the gunshot in her house?"

He nods. "That's her."

"Holy hell," I say.

"But the detective in charge of that missing person's case already ran a thorough investigation. He spoke to her roommate and got statements from her neighbors. He did everything he could to figure out what happened to her and wasn't able to find her or the ambulance that took her," he says.

"Now we know where she ended up," I say. "At least her head. Possibly more of her. We'll have to wait for the medical examiner to confirm which parts belong together."

It sounds macabre and almost dismissive to say it that way, but there's no other way to put it. We have four freezers containing body parts and two that likely did in the recent past. We have to identify which parts go together so we know exactly how many victims we are dealing with right now. But Dr. Perry is the only one who could do that, and it will take time.

"We can run the image of the other head through the missing persons' database to see if there are any hits," he says. "Facial recognition might be able to link us to the right person."

It takes some time to run the image, but by the next morning, we have an answer.

"Valerie Constantine," Detective Cartwright says as he carries a box of records and evidence into the room. "The second head belongs to a woman who went missing about six weeks after Carla Perkins. Her car was found abandoned by the side of the road, but there were never any leads about what happened after she pulled over. The case went cold almost immediately."

"Looks like it's time to warm it back up," I say. "And the Carla Perkins case too. I know that the investigation was thorough, but we need to look into it again. I can interview her roommate again."

"That works," the detective says. "Her name is Olive Willard. I can get you her contact information. I'll look into Valerie while you do that."

I take the contact information he gives me and call Olive Willard.

"Hello?" she answers, sounding wary of the unrecognizable number that came up on her phone screen.

"Olive Willard?" I ask.

"That's me," she says. "Who is this?"

"My name is Dean Steele. I'm a private investigator. I'm working on a case, and I'd really like to talk to you. Would you be able to meet with me for just a few minutes?"

"You're working on a case that I would know something about?" she asks. There's a bewildered pause before she speaks again. "Is this about Carla?"

"I can give you more information when we meet in person," I tell her.

"Okay," she says. "Where do you want to meet?"

"Do you know Thompson's?" I ask, naming the coffee shop where I met with Carson.

"Yeah, I know it," she says. "I can be there in half an hour."

"That works for me," I say. "Thanks."

"We still have the case file for Carla Perkins out here, don't we?" I ask Mason when I get off the phone.

"We should," he says, looking over everything spread across the table. "Yeah, right here."

He hands me the folders, and I sit down with them. I have a little bit of time to go through them again so I'm better prepared for the conversation with Olive. I read over the initial investigation notes and scan the interviews, and then I realize I only have a few minutes and have to leave. Detective Cartwright and I agree to meet back here when I'm finished, and I head out.

The case file included a still from a news interview with Olive, so I'm able to identify her when she comes into the coffee shop a few minutes later. I wave at her from the table, and she comes over without stopping to order a drink. Slinging her purse around the back of the chair, she sits down and meets my eyes without hesitation.

"What do you know about Carla?" she asks.

I extend my hand across the table to her. "Dean Steele."

"Olive," she says, shaking my hand in a way that says she's doing it just to humor me. "This is about Carla, isn't it?"

"It is," I tell her. "I can't give you the full details of everything right now…"

"Why not?" she asks. "I've been waiting for months to find out anything about where she went. If you know something, I want to know."

"I understand how frustrating this is for you," I tell her. "Trust me when I tell you that. But I need you to understand that this is an active investigation and some information needs to be kept among the investigators."

She lets out a heavy sigh. "All right."

"Thank you for your understanding. First, I tried to find any family of hers that I might be able to speak with, but there wasn't anyone listed in the original investigation file. Do you have any contact information for her parents?" I ask.

"Her parents died a few years ago," she tells me. "And she was an only child, so that just left her on her own. That's why I was the first person they talked to about her being missing."

I draw in a breath. Without a next of kin, there's officially no one to give the death notification to. That means I need to tell Olive.

"If that's the case, then I need you to act as next of kin for Carla Perkins," I tell her.

As soon as I say that, her eyes well with tears and her body physically recoils from mine. I regret meeting with her in a public place rather than suggesting that we meet at her house, but I didn't know I would be giving her this news.

"No…," she says, shaking her head.

"Would you rather go somewhere else to talk?" I ask. "We don't have to stay here. We can go to a park or to your place."

Olive draws herself up straighter and squares her chin. She sniffs and lets out a resolute breath. "No, I want to hear this now," she says.

I don't like the idea of giving her this news right here in front of so many people, but it's the option she's choosing. I'm not going to give her the full grisly details. There's no need for her to know that yet.

"I'm very sorry to have to inform you that Carla Perkins is deceased," I tell her. "Remains were found yesterday."

Her hands come up to tent over her mouth, and she draws in a sharp breath. She sits like that, not breathing, not reacting, for several seconds. I wait. She deserves as much time as she needs to process what I just told her. It's obvious she has gone through the last several months believing that her roommate and friend is still alive and that there is hope that she would come back home. Now she is having to face the stark reality that this person she cares so much for is gone.

"What happened?" Olive finally asks.

"We don't have a cause of death yet," I tell her. "And I can't give you the details of the circumstances surrounding her body being found. You'll know as soon as we're able to discuss it. For now, I'm focused on trying to find out what happened to her and who is responsible."

She nods, and I take out my notepad so I can write down what she says.

"What do you want to know?" she asks.

"You weren't at home the night that she went missing," I say. "Where were you?"

"At work," she says. "My schedule had been changed a couple weeks before, and we were still trying to get used to it. Carla wasn't the biggest fan of being alone at night, even though it wasn't late. Even if we weren't actually doing anything together when we were both at the house, she really preferred it when we were there together. I guess just knowing I was in the house made her feel better."

This stands out to me, but I keep going.

"Had you called to check in on her or anything?" I ask.

"No. It was a really busy night at work, and I didn't even stop for a break until the police called to let me know that the alarms had gone off in the house and no one responded to the alarm company when they called. That's when I found out that Carla wasn't in the house and there were signs that she'd been hurt," Olive says.

"When did you find out about the ambulance taking her away from the scene?" I ask.

"The police interviewed the neighbors, and one of them said they heard a loud sound and then saw an ambulance taking her out of the

THE WOMAN IN THE ATTIC

house and putting her in the back. I had some hope then. I thought maybe she'd been hurt but that she was at the hospital and would be fine. Only she wasn't at the hospital. No one could figure out what happened to her," she says.

"You said at the time that she didn't have a boyfriend," I say. "So she wasn't seeing anyone? Did she have a boyfriend anytime close to that?"

"She hadn't had a boyfriend in a long time," Olive says. "She wanted one but just hadn't found anyone who clicked."

"Did she have any hobbies, activities that she did regularly, anything like that?" I ask.

"She volunteered at the hospital."

CHAPTER TWENTY-FOUR

"Carla Perkins volunteered at the hospital," I say, walking back into the room with Detective Cartwright after leaving Thompson's. "And she had a friend who her roommate hadn't met but who Carla had just started talking about. She couldn't remember his name, but she said she thought she met him while volunteering. That has to mean something."

"It might, but I interviewed Valerie Constantine's mother and her best friend, and neither of them mentioned any connection to the hospital. I asked about her work, volunteering, hobbies, all of that, and they didn't mention the hospital or anything to do with it," he says.

"Damn it," I say, sitting down in my chair. "Someone murdered these women and others, and nearly killed Erin, and we can't make any connection. They just killed Melissa Garrison. They're going to kill again if we can't figure out who they are and why they're doing this."

THE WOMAN IN THE ATTIC

The suspicion is still roiling in the back of my mind, but I can't put the pieces together yet. Something is missing, and I don't know where to find it.

"I found out that Valerie was supposed to be going out with friends the night that she went missing. When she didn't show up, her friends called her and didn't get any response, so they called her boyfriend, who also said that he didn't know where she was. She'd told him she was going out with some girls and would call him when she got home later. They were worried she might have gotten into an accident or something, so they retraced her route and found her car. It was on the side of the road but didn't look like it had malfunctioned or anything. It was just sitting there with the door open, and Valerie was missing," he says.

"Where was this?" I ask.

"Next town over," he says. "The detective who handled the case said they were really focused on the boyfriend at first because apparently, they were going through kind of a rough patch. According to her friends, they had been arguing, and Valerie even said she was thinking about leaving him, so the thought was that the boyfriend found out he was about to get the boot and went after her. He somehow got her to pull off on the side of the road to talk to him, and things went wrong."

"But they were never able to prove that?" I ask.

"He had an alibi. He was with a bunch of other people at a movie that night. He couldn't have had anything to do with it, and they weren't able to find anything to suggest he arranged for it to happen or anything. He admitted that they were going through a hard time and that he knew she had been thinking of leaving him, but he insisted that they were working things out and had been on better terms."

"It would be interesting to see what her friends had to say about that," I say. "He might have thought they were doing much better when she had a totally different idea of what was going on. Maybe there was someone else involved, and he didn't know."

Mason's phone rings, and he picks it up from the table.

"Detective Cartwright," he says. He pauses as he listens to the voice on the other end of the line. "Hello, Dr. Perry." Another pause. "How sure are you about that? All right, thank you for calling."

He drops his phone to the table again and sighs heavily, raking his fingers back through his hair, and hangs his head down for a second.

"That was the medical examiner?" I ask.

"Yeah," he says, sitting up and looking over at me. "He's been looking over the body parts, and he says he doesn't think that they go together. He says obviously he can't tell me that with one hundred percent certainty until there are DNA tests performed on the body parts, but he is reasonably certain that the different numbers actually correspond to different victims."

"Which means we're not just looking at a few more victims. We're potentially looking at more than a dozen," I say.

"How could there be that many victims and we didn't know?" he asks.

"Valerie Constantine was from a different area," I say. "They could have been spread around, and right now we haven't identified any clear links between the victims."

"Except the ambulance," he says. "At least in the case of Carla Perkins."

"All the numbers aren't accounted for in the freezers," I say. "And if those body parts don't belong to the same bodies, where are the rest of the remains?"

"We need to do a search of the grounds, see if there are any places where there could be fresh burials," Detective Cartwright says. "We need to find the rest of these victims if we're going to be able to identify them."

He makes the call to have the grounds of the house searched, and when he comes back, I have an idea.

"We should search for any murder cases over the last year in and around Briar Glen that have involved a missing body part. Like Melissa Garrison. Her body was found, but her hand was in that freezer. There might have been other murders where just a part was taken."

Digging into the murders that have occurred over the last year doesn't take long. Briar Glen and the surrounding areas don't experience many murders every year, and the ones that do are generally easily linked to quick explanations like domestic violence. We only get one hit other than Melissa, a woman named Pat Miller, who was found a few weeks before Carla Perkins went missing without one of her legs.

Detective Cartwright and I travel to the next town to talk with Pat Miller's husband. He tells us that his wife had gone on a solo camping and hiking trip, something she did fairly often. She liked being outdoors far more than he did, so he rarely went along with her when she went on these expeditions, which he said was fine with her. She appreciated the solitude and the time to just relax and enjoy being in nature. He knew she was going to be gone for a few days, but when she didn't come home and he couldn't get in touch with her after a couple of days longer than he expected to, he got worried and called the police.

They searched the park where she had gone and found her campsite. Her backpack, hiking boots, and other equipment were missing, which told them that she had left the campsite to go for a hike when she went missing. They immediately thought she had injured herself in a fall or other accident and put out an even larger search.

She wasn't found in the park. It wasn't until two weeks later that her remains were found in a shallow grave on a piece of unused land where a forager happened to be searching for mushrooms. Her leg was missing, and they determined that it had been removed after death.

But it's a detail her husband shares with us about Pat's life before she went on that trip that gets my brain racing. According to him, she was planning on a solo trip for the majority of the time that she was going to be away, but she told him that she might be meeting up with someone during her time out there. A new friend she met while spending time with her sister during an extended time in the Briar Glen hospital.

"We need to go back and talk to Erin McCain," I say to Detective Cartwright when we get back into the car after talking with Pat Miller's husband.

"Why?" he asks.

"I want to find out if she can remember anything else. The doctor said her memories might come back, and she might be able to clarify some of the things she does remember. I need to know more about this EMT she is so worried about," I tell him.

The suspicion has grown in my mind and is pulsating now, swelling in my thoughts and twisting the investigation into something I never would have expected. But I need more information. I need the pieces that are still missing to make sure I'm right and to get the answer to one of the most challenging questions that is ever asked during an investigation:

Why?

I call Ron McCain as we're driving back toward Briar Glen to make sure that it's a good time to visit with Erin.

"She's actually been discharged," he tells me. "We left the hospital a few hours ago and are getting her settled back at home."

"Would it be all right if I came over and talked to her? I know that she's been through a lot and getting back to the house might have been hard on her too, but I really need to see if I can find out any more from her," I say.

"All right, you can come," he says. "But please be gentle with her. She might be acting strong, but all of this has really taken a toll on her. I think she's just now starting to process that Sophie died in our house and she didn't even know it was happening."

"I will take as little time as I can, and if she seems to not want to talk, I'll leave her alone," I promise.

"I think it would be better if I went alone," I tell Detective Cartwright. "I don't know them well, but I have interacted with them more, and she might be more at ease if she's just talking to me."

"That's fine," he says. "I don't have a shortage of things to do for this investigation. I'm going to go back to the investigation room and see if I can find any missing person's reports that fit with our cases."

He drops me off at my car, and I head over to the McCain house.

Ron meets me at the door. "Before you go in, I just wanted to thank you again for arranging the crime scene cleanup team. Knowing that was taken care of takes so much off of me, and I felt worlds better bringing Erin home without having to think about that. She hasn't mentioned wanting to go up into the attic, and I don't know if she will, but I'm glad that it's cleaned up if she does," he says.

"You're welcome," I say. "I'm glad it made you feel better."

His mention of the attic has my fingertips tingling and the hair standing up on the back of my neck. I glance at the steps as he lets me inside, remembering going upstairs in the house and discovering the door to the attic and thinking it would lead to another bedroom. All I can think is how difficult it would be for someone to know where that door was if they didn't know the layout of the house and were in a panic. And how no one would know that if they hadn't been in the house.

Erin is in the living room, propped up on the couch amid sheets and pillows that create a makeshift bed. A cup of water and a plate of fruit sit on the table in front of her, and she's watching TV. She mutes it when I walk into the room.

"You look comfortable," I say with a grin.

She smiles in return and reaches up to touch the pillow behind her head. "Ron is spoiling me. I think he might be going a bit overboard."

"I don't think so," I say. "Not after what you went through." I perch on the edge of a chair and clasp my hands in front of me. "Speaking of which, I really need to talk to you again about what happened the night you were attacked. I'm hoping it's possible you might have come up with some new memories or something might come to you."

The smile fades from her face, replaced by a look of intense concentration.

"I've been trying to think about it. The doctor said the drugs I was given can take away memories or make them fuzzy but that if I keep concentrating, they might come back," she says. "I really want to be able to remember something that will help you."

"I know," I say. "And this isn't your fault. I don't want you to think that I'm angry with you or anything because you can't remember. I'm just trying to make sense of what happened that night, and I think you are the only one who is going to have the pieces I can put together."

"I still don't remember seeing Sophie that night, but sometimes I'll get a flash of something, and I think I heard her voice. I can't remember what she was saying, but I'm pretty sure I heard her."

"All right," I say. "That's something. How about the EMT? Is there anything else about him that you remember? You said that he said he was going to help you. Do you know why he was going to help you?"

She shakes her head. "The only thing I can think of is hitting my head on the counter. Maybe that's what he was going to help me with. Sophie could have called 911 to get help after I hurt myself."

"That's the problem," I tell her. "No one called 911 to get an ambulance to come to this house. We don't know who those EMTs were or how they got to your house."

"Those?" she asks.

"Yeah, Sylvia said that she saw two EMTs at your house."

"I only saw one," Erin tells me. "And he looked so familiar. That just keeps sticking in my mind, how familiar he looked. He was wearing a hat and a mask, so it had to be something about his eyes."

"What color were they?" I ask.

"Hazel," she says. "With a lot of green."

"How about what happened after he told you he was going to help you?" I ask. "Has anything else come back?"

"I still can't remember getting outside. But I know someone was chasing me. I can still feel them right behind me. And I remember hearing a scream."

"A scream?" I ask.

"Yes, I don't know who it was. I guess it might have been me," she says.

I think back on what Keith Cumberland said about being woken up by something, and I wonder if both he and Sylvia were woken up by the same scream Erin heard.

CHAPTER TWENTY-FIVE

Detective Cartwright is on the phone when I get back to the investigation room. He makes eye contact with me and lifts his eyebrows, like he's trying to signal that the conversation is significant. I sit down at the table with him and wait for him to be finished.

"All right. Thanks so much for calling. I really appreciate it. Bye." He ends the call and sets his phone down.

"Who was that?" I ask.

"That was Dr. Perry," he says. "He found something very interesting when he was examining one of the legs that we found in that basement. Either the person who cut it off didn't notice or they were looking for a unique souvenir, but he noticed evidence of a surgical scar on the leg. He said it was really faint, so most people wouldn't think anything of it, but he noticed it and decided to scan the leg to see if there were any medical implants inside. As it turns out, there was."

THE WOMAN IN THE ATTIC

"Did it have an identification number on it?" I ask, feeling excitement building in my stomach.

Medical devices such as implants and replacement joints are generally registered to the person who has them. If he was able to find the number on the device within the leg, we could track down the person that the device was implanted into, identifying our victim.

"There was," he says. "The device was registered to Colleen Frank of Briar Glen."

"That's amazing," I say. "We have another ID."

"Yes, we do. Now let's see if we can find Ms. Frank anywhere in the crime databases. She didn't come up in the search for murders involving body parts being removed, which means she might still be listed as a missing person," he says.

We delve into the missing persons' database, searching for Colleen Frank's name and the details about her that the medical examiner was able to provide. Nothing comes up. Even though she didn't come up in our search for dismembered remains, we search for her in the crime database as well, but we also come up with nothing. This immediately strikes me as odd. She should have come up in one of those. On a whim, I run a search through the search engine of her name and "Briar Glen."

A couple of hits come up, but one draws my attention instantly.

"Here's her obituary," I say. "She died three months ago after an illness."

We look at each other, both baffled by what we're seeing.

"Could this be the wrong Colleen Frank?" Detective Cartwright asks. "Is it possible there were two women by the same name in Briar Glen who died close together?"

"I suppose that's possible, but it doesn't seem very probable considering the size of the town. But all we can do is investigate. We need to contact her family to find out if the Colleen from this obituary had a medical device in her leg."

The obituary lists her mother and her sister as survivors, so we do an online search and come up with the social media profile of her sister. I send a quick message to Lila Frank telling her who I am and that I need to speak with her about her sister's death. I give her my phone number and ask her to get in touch with me when she has free time. It takes only a matter of minutes before she calls.

"Is this the private investigator?" she asks when I answer.

"Yes, it is," I say.

"This is Lila Frank. You sent me a message saying you need to talk to me about my sister," she says.

"Yes," I say. "Thank you for getting in touch with me."

"I don't understand. What would a private investigator need with information about my sister? Is someone saying that she did something?" she asks. "Mr. Steele, with all due respect, I think you might have the wrong person or have been misled. My sister is dead. She has been for three months."

"I know," I tell her. "And I am very sorry for your loss. But I am almost positive I have the right person. It might be easier if could talk face-to-face. Can you do that?"

"I really don't have a lot of time right now," she says.

"Then we'll just talk on the phone," I say quickly, not wanting to encourage her to hang up. "I know this conversation isn't easy for you, and I'm sorry to disrupt your day. I appreciate you getting back to me and being willing to talk. It could be instrumental to a case I'm working on."

"This is all very confusing," she says.

"I know, but I promise I will make sure you have all the information available as soon as possible," I say. "But first, I need to ask you if your sister had any type of medical implant in her body at the time of her death."

"A medical implant?" she asks. "Well, yeah, I mean, she had surgery on her leg, and they had to put some stuff in there."

That might not be exactly precise, but it's enough to tell me what I needed to know. The leg that is now at the medical examiner's office does belong to Lila's sister, Colleen Frank. Now it's just a matter of finding out why the leg of a woman who died of an illness is among the body parts of murder victims.

"And I read in her obituary that she died of an illness?" I ask.

"Yes. Cancer. It happened very quickly," she says.

"All right. This might sound like a very strange question, and again, I apologize, but I need to ask. What happened to your sister's body after her death?"

The obituary didn't list any information about a viewing or the burial, so either it was published very shortly after death and none of that had been arranged yet, or it was purposely kept private due to the wishes of the family. Either way, I can't get those details from the obituary, so I need to find out from Lila.

"What happened to her body?" she asks, sounding horrified.

"Yes," I say.

"She went to Lacey's Funeral Home," she tells me. "And then she was buried."

THE WOMAN IN THE ATTIC

"Ms. Frank, I know you're busy, but I am going to need to meet with you and your mother at your earliest convenience. It is extremely important. I'll have a detective with me," I say.

"What's going on?" she asks.

"I really can't discuss any further details over the phone. I need to meet with both of you in person so I can explain the situation," I say.

"Okay," she says. "You can come to my house. I'll get my mother to meet us in an hour."

I get her address and thank her again before hanging up.

"I just talked to Lila, Colleen Frank's sister," I tell Detective Cartwright when he comes back into the room with coffee for both of us. "She confirmed that her sister did have a medical implant in her leg and that she died from cancer three months ago. She said that her body was brought to Lacey's Funeral Home, and then she was buried."

"Then how did her leg end up in that freezer?" he asks.

"I don't know, but we're meeting with her and her mother in an hour. We're going to have to explain to them what happened. There's only one way to be absolutely sure that the leg belonged to Colleen Frank and the registration number wasn't wrong," I say.

"I don't think there's any question," Mason says.

"I don't either, but we have to be sure."

Lila Frank's expression is drawn when we get to her house. She meets us at the door and stops us before we go inside.

"My mother is still extremely sensitive about my sister," she says.

"I understand," I tell her. "And we don't mean to cause any more pain or difficulty than both of you are already going through. You have to trust that this is extremely important."

"All right, come in."

She leads us through the house into a cozy living room where an older woman is sitting on a couch sipping iced tea. I walk up to her with a smile I hope will help to defuse her tension.

"Hello, I'm Dean Steele. I'm a private investigator. And this is Mason Cartwright. He's a detective with the Briar Glen police," I say.

"Lucy Frank," she says, shaking my hand and then Mason's. "My daughter told me that you need to speak to us about my daughter, Colleen. I don't understand. What could this possibly be about?"

I look to Mason, who gestures to the seat beside Lucy. "May I sit?"

"Go ahead," she says.

He and I both sit down and lean closer to Lucy. She sets her drink down, and I notice her hand is shaking. This whole situation is already having a serious effect on her, and I worry about how she is going to react to the full news of what has happened.

"First, I want to say I am so sorry for the loss of your daughter. I can't imagine how difficult that is," he says.

"That's because it's unimaginable," she says. "No one should have to go through losing a child."

"No, no one should," he says.

"But my daughter died from cancer. Why would that have anything to do with a private investigator or a detective?" she asks.

"Ma'am," I say, "we are working on a case that has become very complicated. I won't share the full details with you, but I'll say that several human remains were found at a location we believe is linked to the investigation into an attack and a murder that happened recently."

"Human remains?" she asks, her hand coming to her chest. "Bodies?"

"Not full bodies," Mason tells her. "Unfortunately, one of the remains we found was a leg containing a medical device registered to your daughter, Colleen."

Her hand moves to her mouth, and her face goes pale. She looks like she might get sick, and I push her drink toward her.

"Take a sip," I tell her. "Take as much time as you need."

She's shaking so hard as she picks up the glass I'm afraid she's going to drop it, but she manages to get a couple of sips before setting it down again.

"Her leg?" she says. "You found her leg?"

"Yes," Mason says. "Right now, that's all that we have confirmed belongs to her. But as you can imagine, we were very confused when we found out that your daughter wasn't murdered and was, in fact, buried after being at the Lacey Funeral Home. We're trying to understand what happened, but we needed to inform you of this finding."

"Thank you," she says. "What are you going to do? What can we do?"

"We need absolute confirmation that this leg does belong to your daughter and there wasn't some mistake," he tells her. "We also need details about how it came to be where we found it. I know this isn't something you want to think about, but I'm asking that you provide permission for us to exhume Colleen."

Lucy draws in a sharp, shuddering breath. She looks over at Lila, who has tears sliding silently down her cheeks. She looks back at us.

"You want to dig my daughter up?" she asks.

"Again, I know this is a lot. This is an extremely difficult thing for you to have to consider, but it could give us crucial information for our investigation," Mason says.

"What about DNA?" Lila asks. "Can't you just take our DNA and test it against the leg to make sure that it is hers?"

"Yes," I say. "We could do that and will need to. That will show that the leg is conclusively Colleen's. But we also need to find out what happened to the rest of her remains. Did you have an open-casket funeral?"

"No. It was open for the visitation but closed for the funeral the next day…" Realization suddenly crosses her face. "You think that someone stole her body after the visitation?"

"We don't know what happened," I say. "Exhuming her body might give us answers. But it's up to you to give us permission."

I know we could go to court and try to get an order to compel the exhumation, but that would take a lot of time we don't have right now. This is a difficult and traumatizing thing to ask of any family, but it could provide valuable insight into what happened to Colleen. It would be far easier if her mother simply gave us permission.

"All right," she finally says softly. "You can do it."

"Thank you," I say. "I promise your daughter will be treated with absolute care and respect."

"Thank you, Mrs. Frank," Mason says.

CHAPTER TWENTY-SIX

Colleen Frank's body is extremely well preserved when the lid of her casket is lifted. The dip in the long skirt of the dress she's wearing is immediately obvious. I look on in horror as Dr. Perry moves the skirt aside and reveals where the leg was removed. The incision looks precise and brutal, like would be found on a butchered animal.

I step back from the casket and turn my back to try to catch my breath. The thought of someone doing this to anyone, but especially to a young woman who had already gone through so much, makes me feel physically ill. Fury rises up in me, and I look at Detective Cartwright, who is staring into the casket with a handkerchief held to his mouth and nose.

"We need to find the son of a bitch who did this to these women," I say.

THE WOMAN IN THE ATTIC

"We need to start with talking to the funeral director," he says. "I'd like to find out why the body of a woman in his care ended up being dismembered before being buried."

We leave the medical examiner's office, and I call Lacey's Funeral Home while we are sitting in the air-conditioned detective's car, trying to catch our breath.

"Hello," I say when someone answers the call. "I'd like to speak to the owner, please."

"Is there something I can help you with?" a woman sounding way too chipper on the other end of the line asks.

"No, thank you. I just need to speak with the owner if they are in," I say.

"Mr. Lacey is in today. I'll see if he is available."

A few moments later, another voice comes through the line.

"Hello? This is Oliver Lacey. I'm the owner and funeral director. How can I help you?" he asks.

"My name is Dean Steele. I was just calling to confirm you are in today. I will be there in a few minutes and would like to speak with you personally about my needs. Would that be possible?" I ask.

"Of course. I'll be here," he says.

"Thank you."

I hang up and look at Detective Cartwright. "He's there and will be waiting for us."

Just as he promised, Oliver Lacey is waiting in the lobby of the funeral home when we arrive. He's wearing an expensive-looking black suit and has a thoughtfully pleasant but reserved expression on his face. This is a man who is a professional at comforting and mourning. He wants to appear welcoming and approachable. But at the same time, he is aware that the people he's usually speaking with are going through incredibly painful and emotionally fraught times, so he also needs to be respectful and subdued.

"Mr. Steele," he says when I walk through the door. "We spoke on the phone."

"Yes, we did," I say. "Thank you for taking the time to talk with me. This is my colleague, Detective Mason Cartwright."

Oliver Lacey's face drops as the detective takes out his badge to show him.

"Do you have some time to come with us so we can have a word with you?" Mason asks.

"What is this about? I thought you were coming in to discuss funeral needs," he says.

"Not exactly," Mason says. "We need to discuss a former client with you. Colleen Frank."

As of right now, we don't have enough to take him into custody or even compel him to speak with us if he doesn't want to. All we can do is bring him in for questioning, which could easily result in him asking for a lawyer and us not getting a single detail out of him. We need to keep him as calm as possible and try to get him to talk to us as much as he can.

"I see," he says. "I suppose I can come with you. Just give me one moment to check something in my office, and I will be right out."

He holds up a finger to further emphasize that he will be back, then scurries down the hallway in front of us. I get a bad feeling as he goes into the office and closes the door behind him. I start toward the door and have only taken a few steps when a loud sound makes me involuntarily duck down. My heart pounds in my chest as I look back at Mason.

"That was a gunshot," I say.

"Go!" he says.

I run down the hallway to the office door and try it. It's locked. I plant a hard kick right next to the doorknob and hear the wood begin to splinter. Another kick breaks the door open completely, and I rush inside. Oliver Lacey is draped over his desk, a gun in his hand and blood trickling from his temple.

"Shit!" I shout. Detective Cartwright comes into the room. "He's dead. He shot himself."

"Damn it," he says.

A woman I'm assuming is the one I spoke to on the phone is running down the hallway, and I rush out to stop her, grabbing her by her shoulders and leading her backward up the hallway so she doesn't look inside the office.

"Ma'am, I'm going to need you to stay back," I say. "Please, just step back and let us handle this."

"What's going on? What was that sound?" she asks.

"It was a gunshot," I tell her. "Mr. Lacey has shot himself."

She lets out a short scream and covers her mouth, reaching for the wall to hold her up. I help her over to a chair and set her down. I can hear Mason in the office calling dispatch. He comes out of the room and shakes his head at me.

"We were so close."

"Apparently too close," I tell him.

THE WOMAN IN THE ATTIC

"Do you think Lacey did this?" Mason asks as Lacey's body is being loaded onto a gurney, covered with a sheet, and brought out to the waiting ambulance.

"No," I tell him. "At least not alone. Remember, there were two EMTs, and they were strong enough to kill multiple women, load them on gurneys, and carry their bodies. I don't think someone as old as Oliver Lacey had it in him to do something like that."

"He obviously provided a body part," Mason says.

"Yes, he did. And possibly more than one."

"What do you mean?" he asks.

"Dr. Perry said that each of the numbered parts was probably from a different victim. But we haven't been able to track that many murders or missing people that fit with the description of the parts. What if the ones we can't link came from here?" I ask.

"What are you thinking?"

"There have to be records of the clients that Lacey handled. We need to have Perry tell us the approximate age of those body parts as well as any other details he can give us about them so we can compare them to the people who came through here in that time frame," I say.

"That could work," he tells me.

By the next afternoon, we have a stack of files, one for each of the body parts Dr. Perry examined. They are like the files that we found in the basement, only providing actual information rather than jumbled code we can't decipher. Mason and I pore over them, trying to find anything that stands out. There are some obvious consistencies about the deaths, including that they are all women, white, and with an estimated height that varies only by an inch.

It's difficult to decide how we are going to reach out to the families of more potential victims of the gruesome funeral director. This is almost as hard as doing a death notification. These people already know that their loved one is dead, but bringing this information to them will only open that wound again and make them suffer a whole new blow. It isn't something I want to do, but we've come this far. We need to know what else we're dealing with.

The funeral home has a "Closed" sign on the door when we arrive to go through the records. The office door is closed, and the woman, who we learn is the receptionist and assistant to Mr. Lacey, Agnes, gestures at it when we walk in.

"You can go ahead," she says.

"Do you know how to access the records?" I ask.

"Of course," she says. "That was part of my job."

"If we gave you specific parameters, could you give us the names and family contact information for the clients who fit that?" I ask.

"Yes," she says.

"That would be amazing," I say.

It saves us from having to go into the office and try to dig through the records ourselves. She's not asking for a warrant, which saves us even more time and hassle. The only difficulty will come if any of the families are angered by their information being released. But considering the service we are trying to fulfill right now, I don't think we're going to have to deal with any of that.

We know that he wouldn't have recorded his clients based on things like race or age, but we're able to narrow down the field to just the women from the last six months. She prints out the information, and we thank her profusely before leaving. I'm relieved when I walk out of the funeral home into the heat of the day.

"Got a bit of a chill?" Mason asks.

"Something like that," I say.

I don't want to think about the disrespect and disregard Oliver Lacey showed Colleen Frank when he removed her leg after her visitation, and what else we might find in the file sitting on my lap as make our way back to the police station. But I have to. This is getting us somewhere. I don't know where yet, but we're getting closer.

There's a small envelope sitting on the table when we get into the investigation room when we get back.

"What's that?" Mason asks.

I shrug and open it. I tip out into my palm, and a couple of small pictures fall out.

"These must be the pictures that were missing from that file," I say.

THE WOMAN IN THE ATTIC

"Great, we'll look into that in a bit. I want to start going through these. It's going to take a while," he says.

I sit down at the table, and we start to go through the files, narrowing down the options by removing the ones that clearly don't fit based on the images included that appeared as memorials during the visitations. Finally, we're left with a handful of files that specify closed caskets or no services. I'm particularly intrigued by the ones that say the women were cremated before their funerals. It's time to start making phone calls.

We decide that it will be more efficient to discuss the possibility of their loved ones being involved in this horrifying situation with multiple families at once, rather than trying to have individual meetings.

The next morning, we gather several of the families. We bring them into one of the conference rooms, and Mason stands in front of them, introducing himself.

"I want to tell you first that we really appreciate you being here and understand that this is a very difficult situation for all of you. Talking about your loved ones is a sensitive issue, and we understand that this is not easy for any of you. This situation, especially, is challenging. If at any point you need to take a break or need to step out of the room, please let us know.

"Recently, Mr. Steele and I have been investigating a case that has become far more complex as it has developed. Information we received led us to the discovery of multiple incomplete human remains. We have been able to identify one of those as belonging to a woman whose body was handled by the Lacey's Funeral Home after her death."

There are a few gasps around the room as people start to catch on to what he's telling them.

"We believe there is a possibility that your loved ones could also have been affected."

There's an outburst among the family members gathered at the table. Several shout out while others burst into tears. Mason looks overwhelmed, so I step in to try to bring the conversation back under control.

"Excuse me," I say, holding my hands out to try to calm them. "I'm Dean Steele. As Detective Cartwright mentioned, I have been helping him on this case. We know this is shocking information to hear, and we don't blame you for being upset. But we do need you to try to keep your composure so we can discuss the details and determine the next steps in this situation. Please."

They begin to settle down, and Mason steps back in to explain further.

"We are not positive right now. We need to run DNA tests to determine if the remains are connected to you," he says.

"My daughter was cremated," one of the mothers says. "How could you have any of her remains?"

"That's something we are still trying to figure out," Mason says. "This is still very much an active and developing situation. Right now, we are just asking for your cooperation in collecting the information."

CHAPTER TWENTY-SEVEN

KNOWING IT WILL TAKE DAYS, IF NOT LONGER, FOR THE DNA we collect from the family members to be processed and compared with the DNA from the body parts, we turn our attention back to the files. There are two pictures of a woman that the team found in the basement. But they don't look like the others. First of all, there are two of them, whereas the other files only had one picture attached. The pictures are also shots from the chest up of a smiling woman with dark blond hair and delicate shoulders. She looks fairly small, but the pictures aren't enough to give all that information.

"She's listed as number 1, but none of the body parts we found in the basement are labeled as 1," I point out.

"And she definitely looks alive in those pictures," Detective Cartwright says. "None of the other pictures have a living person in them."

"Whoever's doing this might have changed their tactics after the first victim," I say. "We need to find out who this woman is and what happened to her."

As I examine the pictures further, I realize I'm not looking at a picture of one woman but of two very identical ones, save for the little birthmark under the lower lip of one of the women. It's faint and almost imperceptible, but there definitely is a birthmark on the one woman's chin that's not in the other picture. I show it to Cartwright, and we decide to run the pictures of the women through the missing persons' database, just as we did with the pictures of the other women's faces.

We're hoping the facial recognition software will be able to pick them out and tell us who they are. Nothing comes back. Confused, we put the pictures through a basic image search online, wondering if it's possible that there are other pictures of each of them that just didn't get picked up in the missing persons' database. Instead, we find another obituary.

"Beverly Hollis," Detective Cartwright reads, showing me a picture of the woman without the birthmark. "Died almost five years ago. It just says 'suddenly,' no explanation."

"Look, there's an article about her," I point out in the search results.

He pulls up the article and reads through it. "It says that she died in what the police called a relatively minor car accident but that she had actually had a heart attack that caused her to lose control of her vehicle. She died in the hospital after." He looks over at me. "Regional Memorial."

"The closed hospital?" I ask.

"That would be the one," he says.

"That's interesting," I say. "What else does it say?"

"Nothing really. She is survived by her children."

Light seems to burst in my mind, and I stand up straighter.

"Her children?" I ask.

"Yeah. It doesn't say anything else about them. Just that her children were devastated by her loss and didn't want to participate in the article," he tells me. "Oh shit. Look. It says that her visitation was planned for Lacey's Funeral Home."

I start to pace back and forth, thoughts racing as things start to fall into place in my mind.

"What is it?" he asks. "What's going on?"

"I need to find out what happened to Sophie Berman's body," I say.

"What do you mean, what happened to her body?" he asks.

"Where did it go? What happened to it? Was it cleared and released to Carson? Does the medical examiner still have it in custody because of the ongoing case?" I ask.

"I can call Dr. Perry and find out," he says.

"Do that. Thanks."

THE WOMAN IN THE ATTIC

We don't find any other search results for the other woman, so while he calls the medical examiner's office, I go back through everything we've already figured out. Words keep repeating at the back of my mind:

"How would she have found that door?"

There are still fragments missing, but the pieces are coming together. It's starting to unravel. The call with the medical examiner only takes a few moments and comes back with the exact information I thought it would.

Sophie's body was cleared and transferred from the medical examiner's office to Lacey's Funeral Home.

As soon as he says that, I'm out the door. I don't bother to wait for him to get in my car and head for the funeral home. I'm on the phone with Agnes as soon as I pull out of the parking lot of the police station.

"Agnes, this is Dean Steele," I tell her. "I'm on my way to the funeral home. I need your help with one more thing."

"All right," she says. "What can I help you with?"

"How far back do your records go?" I ask. "Would you be able to find one for me from five years ago?"

"Yes, I should be able to do that," she says.

"Great. Could you please look up Beverly Hollis? Print out everything you can find on her for me."

"I'll have it ready for you when you get here," she says.

"Thank you, Agnes," I say.

She still sounds like she's getting over the shock of what happened to Oliver Lacey right there in the place where they'd been working together for decades. I know she's grappling with not only his suicide but with the reality of what he had been doing with the bodies of people entrusted to him by their families in some of their most vulnerable moments. As of right now, the funeral home is still open, and the media hasn't gotten hold of the full story. They reported his suicide but didn't go into any detail about the circumstances that led up to it.

For now, we're trying to keep the information about the body parts as contained as possible, but that's not going to last for very long. With all the families that we've contacted and are working with to conclusively identify the body parts that were likely taken from the funeral home, it's going to get out and end up splashed everywhere soon enough.

My phone starts ringing the second I end the call with Agnes. It's Mason Cartwright.

"Where did you go?" he asks.

"I'm on my way to Lacey's Funeral Home," I tell him. "I'm getting all the information on her that I can get from their records. And I'm going to check to make sure that Sophie's body didn't just skim under the radar and is actually there."

"What are you doing after that?" he asks.

"I'm not sure. I'll keep you posted."

I end the call shortly before pulling into the parking lot of the funeral home. The rest of the lot is empty except for a car I'm assuming belongs to Agnes. She is behind the welcome desk, just like she was the last time I was here. Everything looks like she's carrying on exactly as she did when Oliver Lacey was in the office at the end of the hallway. I wonder if she tells herself he still is.

"Mr. Steele," she says when she sees me. "I have that information for you."

"Thank you, Agnes," I say. "How are you holding up?"

She shakes her head, tears pooling in her eyes. "I got a call today from a woman asking me if her daughter was actually cremated or if she should worry that something happened to her. I didn't know what to tell her. I don't know how she heard about what Oliver did or who else she's told."

"Don't answer the phone," I tell her. "Detective Cartwright told you about the investigation into practices here, and I need you to understand. It is about to get far more intense and complicated. I don't want you talking to anybody about it, all right? Right now, as much needs to be kept confidential as possible, so if anyone else calls, just let it go to voice mail. I suggest recording a new message directing anyone with questions to contact the detective."

Mason likely isn't going to be happy at the prospect of getting so many calls from people who have heard about the missing leg or any of the other families wanting to know if the same fate had befallen their own loved ones. It seems the information has already leaked, and there's no stopping the questions and morbid curiosity now. But that's the furthest thing from my mind. I don't care how many people are asking questions, as long as I find the answers.

I look down at the paper that she gave me, and a shock of electricity goes through me.

"Agnes, can you answer one more question for me?" I ask.

"If I can," she says.

"Have you received the body of Sophie Berman for burial?" I ask. "She should have come within the last few days."

"No," she says. "We haven't gotten any women in more than a week. That might be something that Oliver was handling." Her voice gets thin and high as she says it, and she presses a tissue she produces from the sleeve of her lightweight sweater to her face.

"I'm sorry," I tell her. "I didn't mean to upset you. I really appreciate your help."

I know things are about to get extremely difficult for Agnes. Without Oliver Lacey alive, the most heat will be coming down on her in the course of investigating the limbs, and I don't know how she's going to handle it. I doubt she had anything to do with them. I don't know if anyone else did.

A little research while I was trying to sleep at Kent and Sylvia's house revealed that Lacey wasn't just the funeral director; he was the mortician. He handled all aspects of the body preparation, as well as the visitations and funeral arrangements. Agnes only helped with the customer service and business end of things. That means he had all the freedom to do whatever he wished with the bodies. The thought is chilling, and I still have the question of why he was willing to do it. But I am going to find out.

I rush back out to my car, and as I'm getting ready to turn it on, a thought comes to my mind. I suddenly remember the homeless man in the abandoned hospital. His rantings didn't seem to make much sense at the time. He raved about telling the others that it was his place, that he had told the doctor and the nurses that it was his. Suddenly, it makes much more sense now.

I pull out my phone and search for Regional Memorial again. The website has been largely stripped down now that the hospital is no longer open, but I am searching for something very specific. It takes me a minute, but I find it. Typing the address into the GPS, I head to the outskirts of town.

Detective Cartwright answers his phone on the first ring.

"What did you find out?" he asks when I've barely gotten a greeting out.

"Sophie's body never made it to the funeral home. But Beverly Hollis's did. She was cremated five years ago under the instructions of her son, Carson Berman."

"Sophie's brother?" he asks, sounding shocked by the revelation.

"I am on my way to the Regional Memorial Emergency Services Clinic," I tell him. "Look up the address, and meet me there."

"The what?" he asks.

"Regional Memorial had an annexed facility while it was operational. It was specifically for emergency services. It's closed too, but I don't think that means it isn't being used. Remember what the homeless man we found in the hospital said about telling all the others that it was his place? I think that means that those others found their own place," I say.

"Dean, don't go inside," he says. "You need to wait for backup."

"I'll meet you there," I say.

I don't commit to what he's saying because I know I'm not going to follow his instructions. I'm positive now that the doctor and the nurses that the man from the hospital was talking about weren't actual medical staff. They told him that they were, but he pushed them away, and it led to them going to this facility. I need to know what's going on inside.

CHAPTER TWENTY-EIGHT

I GET TO THE CLOSED EMERGENCY FACILITY AND DRIVE UP THE abandoned entryway to the entrance. It's boarded up, so I continue driving around until I see a side door with a padlocked chain securing it. The image of the gate in front of the house in the woods flashes through my mind. I stop my car and climb out. Going to the trunk, I get the bolt cutters I've started keeping there and carry them to the door. I don't have time to try to remove the lock or find another way inside. Breaking through the chain, I drop the bolt cutters on the ground and pull the door open.

A gust of stale air comes out at me. The building has few windows, and those are covered, leaving the interior inky dark. Scooping up the bolt cutters off the ground, I go back to my trunk and toss them in, grabbing the flashlight before closing it and jogging back inside the facility. I'm not positive about what I'm looking for, but I know something is here. Carson Berman uses this space for something. He and his sister collected those body parts for a reason, and I am going to find out why.

Delving deeper into the building, I swing the flashlight into each of the rooms I walk past. Like in the abandoned hospital, some of the rooms still contain remnants of the facility's past. Beds, dressers, and old equipment sit waiting for patients that won't come, doctors who had left and won't be returning. Following my instincts, I continue into the building until I find a stairwell that brings me down to a short gate blocking off another door. I climb over the gate and try the door. It's unlocked, letting me into the basement. I hope this is what I'm looking for.

Walking through the basement, I shine the flashlight on the walls until I finally see a door marked "Morgue."

Taking a breath, I walk up to the door and take hold of the handle. I notice a slight glow behind the curtain covering the window in the door and realize there are lights on inside the room. The building could still have limited access to electricity, but I assume it has a generator, much like the one concealed outside the house in the woods. I walk into the room and am immediately hit by a wall of cold that can't cover a sickening smell.

There's a gurney with a sheet draped over a shape on it sitting on the side of the room. I'm starting toward it when the door across the room opens and Carson Berman steps out toward me. He's wearing scrubs and gloves, a mask down under his chin. There's a slight smile on his face as he eyes me.

"Well done, Dean," he says. "I underestimated you. I didn't think you would be able to figure it out. I have to thank you for how sympathetic and compassionate you were with me when you had to inform me of my sister's death. It really did make a difference during that difficult time."

"You killed her," I say.

He shakes his head. "No, that's the thing. It truly was an accident. And it was a shock when I found out. Your comforting meant a lot to me."

The words make my skin crawl as I realize I not only tried to comfort and reassure this man after his sister's death but also asked for his help during the investigation. He knew what I was doing and followed along like he was watching a TV show.

"Why was she in the attic?" I ask. "You said you didn't even know how she would have found the door."

"A slip. I thought it would sound like I was more confused, but then I realized it actually told you exactly what you wanted to know. That I was the one in the house with them that night. I don't know why she was in the attic. She said she was going to hide upstairs in case Erin

McCain got away from me, but I can't imagine why she would go up into the attic."

"Because she didn't know that door led to it," I say. "It must have locked behind her when she got inside."

"A tragedy," he says.

"And all for nothing." The sound of another voice makes me whip around.

A man is at the door wearing a doctor's coat and gloves.

"Dean, meet my father, Anthony Hollis," he says.

"Your father?" I ask, shaking my head. "But you were listed as Sophie's next of kin. If he's your father, he would have been listed."

"Technically, he's my stepfather, but he's the only father I've ever known. The man who conceived Sophie and me with our mother left before she was born, and I was too young to have any memories of him. We had no one until Anthony came along," he says. "And he taught us everything."

"Why weren't you mentioned in the article about your wife's death?" I ask, feeling the tingle at the back of my neck that says something much bigger than I realized is happening.

"We were going through a divorce at the time. Something I didn't want and I don't believe that she truly did either. We'd gone through a hard time, but it wasn't enough to end our love story. We were going to work it out. I know we were."

He walks forward toward Carson and the covered gurney, making me turn swiftly so I can keep my eyes on him.

"But we never had the chance. And it was my fault."

"How was it your fault?" I ask. "She had a heart attack and was in a car accident."

"I could have saved her. She was brought to the hospital on a day when I should have been there, but I'd taken the day off. I should have been there when she needed me, and I would have been able to save her. I would have made sure she lived, and then we could have been together again. But it's all right. Soon we will be again. I've waited five years, but soon I'll have my love again."

He walks up to the gurney and pulls back the sheet. I recoil in horror at the sight of body parts sewn together into a new corpse lying on the table. The source of the smell is now obvious, and I fight to keep my stomach from revolting. My eyes are drawn to the face of the patched-up corpse, and I see the face of the woman with the birthmark. Beverly's almost exact replica.

"It's taken me five years for my plan to be complete. You see, I'm going to bring her back to life."

"Carson had her cremated," I say.

"No," Carson explodes. "I never authorized that. Oliver made a mistake, and he cremated my mother. We never signed the papers. He made the mistake. It was his fault."

"It's all right, son," Anthony says soothingly. "I know you didn't do it. And it worked out. Oliver turned out to be extremely helpful when I realized there was another way to bring my beloved back. If I could just find the right parts, I could create her again. We worked so hard to find every part we needed. We even found extras just in case there was a problem. This is a new science, after all. A medical miracle."

"It's impossible," I tell him. "You can't bring *this* back to life."

He strokes the head on the pieced-together body and gazes down at it like he truly is looking at his wife.

"Are you a doctor, Dean?" he asks.

"No," I tell him.

"Then you can't possibly understand."

"Where is Sophie?" I ask.

Anthony walks up to the wall of drawers and pulls one out, revealing Sophie's body lying on the slab.

"I had to protect her. I'm going to bring her back too, and then we can be a family. But I can't do that if you are in my way," he says.

Too late, I realize Carson has moved around behind me. I turn to face him and see him coming at me with a scalpel.

He dives at me, swiping at my neck, and I lean back away as best I can. It knicks my shoulder and tears through the fabric of my thin shirt. I don't even feel the rip of my skin in the adrenaline that dumps through my system, and I throw a jab, hard, into the passing body of Carson's face. It connects with his chin, and he stumbles with momentum.

"Get him," I hear Anthony say somewhere behind me as Carson gets his feet under him again.

I'm not worried about Anthony getting involved, at least not yet, so I focus completely on Carson. He is a pretty well-built guy, but he doesn't seem terribly athletic.

As he rights himself and lunges again, I weave out of the way and pepper him with two shots to the ribs. He lets out a furious and frustrated groan and swings the scalpel backward at head level. I duck and slam my fist into his stomach again, realizing only too late that I've opened myself up.

THE WOMAN IN THE ATTIC

A piercing pain goes into my shoulder blade as the scalpel digs in, and Carson wriggles it around viciously. I let out a shout of pain and shove forward, pushing him back into the wall of slabs. Standing quickly, I break his hold on the knife in my back and grab his head with both hands, slamming the side of his face into the open slab his sister lies in.

I don't wait for him to react, slamming my elbow into his nose and shifting my feet to get a better stance when he begins to buckle. Putting as much power as I can into my right hand, I punch him hard in the stomach, then uppercut his cheek. My left arm feels useless, and I can feel the blood trickle down my back, but I have him stunned and staggering back into the wall of drawers. Now is my chance to put him out.

I take a step back and then kick hard, the heel of my foot slamming into his stomach again, sending him buckling over sideways. He bangs his head on the slab again, and blood pours from a wound on his forehead, and I kick again at his shoulder. When he slumps to the ground, I have to pull myself back.

Before I can turn, I sense something behind me. I clench my body as Anthony Hollis dives onto my back. The scalpel still sticking out of my shoulder is driven deeper into me, and I fall to my knees with him on top of me.

"You shouldn't be here!" he shouts as he yanks the blade out of my back.

I crumple to the ground and roll so I can face him. He raises the scalpel high over his head, holding on to the handle with both hands, one wrapped around the other.

There's only a split second to react, but my instincts and training kick in. As he dives down toward me, I open my legs and catch him, using my hands to catch his and my right leg to break the hold of his left arm. He's older and weaker than I am, and the ax-kick motion breaks his grip easily, allowing me to wrap that leg around his neck and bring my ankles together, bringing him into a triangle choke.

He bats at me with his free arm, but my hands are working on his fingers, getting the weapon away from him. When he finally releases it, he lets out a furious scream for his son, and I smash my fist into his mouth. A second one breaks his nose, and I feel it crunch under me, blood exploding out of his face and down his cheek.

But the choke is tight, and slowly, he begins to lose his fight. He slumps down to the ground, and I can see his eyes fluttering closed. He is mumbling, cursing at me, but spittle is stuck on his bloody lips, the red so brilliant in the bright lights of the operating lamps.

In the distance, I can hear shouting, and I know it's the backup arriving. I want to relax and just hold on to Anthony, but I can see Carson stirring against the wall. Anthony is less of a threat, especially now. I have to let him go.

Releasing Anthony, I scramble to my feet and am met by a surprisingly hard right hand to the jaw from Carson. He wobbles as I try to reorient myself, and I realize he's only partially there. I lunge at him but slip on something wet and careen into his midsection. He slams his fist down on my wounded shoulder, and I crumple in pain at his feet. He does it again, and the adrenaline soars through my veins.

I grab his right leg and lunge, a single-leg takedown making him stumble backward. His head smashes on the wall of slabs behind him. He makes a sound that almost sounds like a mumbling snore, and I let go of his leg to plant another hard right on his jaw. A second and third land without a defense, and I stop myself from throwing a fourth.

Staring into the glassy eyes of Carson Berman, I drop my right hand just as the door behind me opens and the shouts of the backup officers fill the room. I fall to my bottom and watch as they leap into action, cuffing both the father and son, and the detective shouts.

"What in fresh hell is this?" the detective demands when he sees the gruesome patchwork body on the gurney.

"Meet Anthony Hollis," I say. "Beverly's estranged husband. I'll explain everything, but get both of them out of here."

One of the officers cuffs Anthony and pulls him to his feet. Anthony struggles, forcing the officer to step to the side enough so that he can lean down and kiss the patchwork body's forehead. The officer yanks him away and drags him out of the room right behind Carson.

"There's the doctor and one of the nurses that the homeless man was ranting about," I tell him. I look back at the body. "Sick, twisted bastards."

CHAPTER TWENTY-NINE

"I SURVIVED BECAUSE IT WAS A MISTAKE TO BEGIN WITH?" Erin asks, looking bewildered.

I'm sitting in the living room of the McCain house with Ron and Erin, trying to explain what I've gotten out of Carson and Anthony since bringing them into custody yesterday. I can't blame her for sounding as confused as she does. It's so much to take in and a horrific thought to realize why she went through what she did.

"Yes," I tell her. "According to Anthony, you were never the actual target. Carson and Sophie were supposed to go after Melissa Garrison, but they misunderstood the instructions and got their wires crossed. Anthony said it was just another mistake he had to fix, and he did."

Erin looks over at Ron, who is sitting across from her in one of the chairs while she sits on the couch. He had told her all about his affair with Melissa so that the information wouldn't come as a shock to her when I had to mention it. There's an icy tension between them right now, and I don't know what's going to happen moving forward, but I find myself hoping that maybe there's a chance for them. If for nothing else than to give Erin continued support as she heals and tries to move forward.

If there isn't, Ron has no one to blame but himself, and he will have to deal with the repercussions. For now, Detective Cartwright and I are still wading through the mind-bending statements that both men have made, trying to make any sense out of what they've said. I know there's really no sense to be made out of some of it—not by someone in their right mind, anyway.

"Sophie's death really was an accident. She locked herself in the attic and was likely trying to figure a way out when she fell on the fire poker. Carson was chasing you, so there was no one to know where she went."

"What happened to Carson?" Erin asks. She shudders. "I still can't believe it was them." She shakes her head. "Why did he just leave the ambulance?"

"When he was in the woods with you, Anthony Hollis called him, and he realized the mistake he'd made. He thought you were already too far gone to be saved, but Anthony didn't want any of your body, so he left you in the woods, in his mind, to die. But by that point, the ambulance had already been noticed, and he knew that it was being watched. He couldn't find Sophie, but his father was insisting that he come back to the emergency facility right then. He tried to explain that he didn't know where Sophie was, but Anthony was too agitated by another mistake made and more problems being caused and told him he was coming to get him.

"He didn't realize that the only people who had seen the ambulance at that point still thought it was completely legitimate and were just worried about what was going on with Erin. If he had taken it, no one would ever have been able to link it to the case. But he was so afraid of his stepfather and so positive that the man knew everything and could not be confronted that he did what he said and walked through the woods until he came out on the street and was picked up. Anthony said they were going to go back for the ambulance, but he thought it was more likely that they would be caught if they did, so they left it knowing it wasn't registered to them and couldn't be traced."

"One more little mistake," Erin says bitterly.

"But one that ensured we were able to find you," I say. "If Sylvia hadn't been worried about that ambulance, we never would have gone inside the house looking for you and found Sophie and realized you weren't there. By the time we noticed that you were missing, you would have been gone."

THE WOMAN IN THE ATTIC

"I really can't thank you enough for all that you did," she says. "I am literally alive because of you."

"I'm glad that Sylvia was as curious as she was and willing to come over and look the way she did," I say. "I believe a lot of lives were saved because of that."

I don't get into the details about that belief with her. She doesn't need to hear that Anthony admitted he had already had to replace some of the body parts on the pieced-together corpse and understood that his efforts to "bring her back to life" might not work the first time, so he had the other parts in reserve for if they were needed. I have no doubt that he would have continued to justify finding women he thought resembled his wife or had characteristics that were like hers and killing them or stealing their body parts from the funeral home if we hadn't stopped him now.

I leave Erin and Ron's house and go back to Kent and Sylvia's. I'm staying one more day and then heading back home. It feels like it has been so long since I've been in my own bed and seen my family. I am looking forward to putting this behind me. I know there's still a lot of work to be done, including tracking down the identities of the dismembered human remains, starting with the woman with the birthmark. And I'll have to be involved in much of it. But for now, I can go home to Harlan and then to Sherwood and take some time to decompress.

Two days later, I'm in Harlan with Xavier having a video call with Emma, Sam, and Owen.

"We checked the key that was on Sophie's body, and it was to the lock in the emergency facility," I tell them. "If I don't miss my guess, I'm assuming the three of them didn't stay inside together very often. They probably had two of them go inside, and then the third locked the padlock again so that if security came by, it would look like everything was fine. They were planning on going to the facility after Erin McCain's house, and it was Sophie's turn to lock the padlock behind her brother and stepfather. Since they were planning on moving a body that day, they would want the two with the greatest strength to be able to carry it down the steps to the morgue."

"What happened to the rest of the bodies that you didn't find in the freezers?" Owen asks. "Did they find them in the search of the property?"

"No," I tell him. "They were cremated by Oliver Lacey and disposed of. "The only parts they kept were the ones that Anthony Hollis thought would recreate his estranged wife."

"He was a doctor," Emma says. "How could he think that he would be able to bring her back to life at all, much less by using parts of other people?"

"He believed her ashes held her essence and that by putting them inside the body, it would regenerate into her, just with a new form. He is a brilliant man, but very broken. He was able to manipulate and influence Carson and Sophie because they were so devoted to him when he came along to, as they saw it, rescue them after their father had left and then even more devoted after their mother died."

"It's just so messed up," Sam says. "I'm glad you stopped him."

"So am I," I say. "I'm hoping the DNA results come through soon so we can conclusively show to whom all the parts in the freezers belonged. I want to be able to return them to their families and finally let them fully grieve. The families that have gotten the results have been so grateful. I can't even imagine what all of this has been like for them."

"I'm guessing Lacey's Funeral Home is closed permanently," Emma says.

"Yes," I tell her. "Agnes is cooperating fully. I really don't believe she knew anything about what was going on. I think Oliver was doing all of it with only the family helping him and she didn't know. This has to be extremely hard on her. She worked with Oliver for so many years. She thought she knew him. She was devastated when he killed himself, and now she's having to cope with finding this out about him."

"Hopefully she'll be all right."

We talk for a little longer, then get off the call. Xavier scurries upstairs and comes down with a big box.

"What's that?" I ask.

"I got you something while you were away," he says.

He hands me the heavy box, and I open it to reveal a pair of roller skates.

"Roller skates?" I ask.

He nods. "Now you can be on my roller derby team."

"Fantastic," I tell him. I look down at the skates for a few seconds, then sit down and start putting them on. "You ready for a round?"

Xavier's face lights up, and he snatches his own skates off the floor so he can put them on. I haven't been on skates in a long time, but it's

THE WOMAN IN THE ATTIC

fine. Right now, scooting around the house after Xavier and occasionally running into the furniture is all I need.

There are still so many questions waiting to be answered.

Horrors waiting to be untangled.

For now, I'll take this and delve back into the rest as it comes.

AUTHOR'S NOTE

Dear Reader,

Thank you so much for choosing to read *The Woman in the Attic*, the ninth book in the Dean Steele Mystery Thriller series! Your positive feedback on the last installment has been incredibly encouraging as we dive deeper into this new season.

So, what did you think of the final reveal of the case? When I came up with the concept, I knew it was pretty dark and a bit creepy. The idea of a former surgeon turning his grief and guilt into such a macabre mission struck me as both tragic and horrifying. And trying to recreate a loved one by collecting and sewing together parts from different people – it's like something out of a real-life horror story or a classic gothic tale like Frankenstein.

I always love hearing your feedback. If you could please take a moment to leave a review for The Woman in the Attic, I would be enormously grateful. Your feedback helps shape Dean's future adventures and ensures that I continue to deliver the thrilling mysteries you love.

In the next installment, *Playing with Fire*, Dean faces a series of mysterious fires and an unidentifiable burnt victim. As he searches for clues, he discovers that the town is teeming with suspects, each with their own motives. Get ready for a rollercoaster of suspense, twists, and unexpected connections!

If you're craving another gripping mystery, I hope you consider joining Dean's cousin, FBI Agent Emma Griffin, in her latest adventure, *The Girl in the Dark*. In this story, years after Luisa Sinclair's disappearance, a fisherman discovers her remains in an ominous drum barrel, reigniting the cold case. As Emma investigates, she uncovers a trail of missing young girls that may be connected. With a cunning predator on the loose, it's a race against time before another innocent life is lost. This gripping murder mystery, will captivate you from the first page to the last!

Thank you for your support and for joining me on this journey. I can't wait to hear your thoughts and have you alongside Dean on his next adventure in *Playing with Fire!*

Yours,
A.J. Rivers

P.S. If for some reason you didn't like this book or found typos or other errors, please let me know personally. I do my best to read and respond to every email at aj@riversthrillers.com

P.P.S. If you would like to stay up-to-date with me and my latest releases I invite you to visit my Linktree page at *www.linktr.ee/a.j.rivers* to subscribe to my newsletter and receive a free copy of my book, Edge of the Woods. You can also follow me on my social media accounts for behind-the-scenes glimpses and sneak peeks of my upcoming projects, or even sign up for text notifications. I can't wait to connect with you!

ALSO BY
A.J. RIVERS

Emma Griffin FBI Mysteries

Season One
Book One—The Girl in Cabin 13*
Book Two—The Girl Who Vanished*
Book Three—The Girl in the Manor*
Book Four—The Girl Next Door*
Book Five—The Girl and the Deadly Express*
Book Six—The Girl and the Hunt*
Book Seven—The Girl and the Deadly End*

Season Two
Book Eight—The Girl in Dangerous Waters*
Book Nine—The Girl and Secret Society*
Book Ten—The Girl and the Field of Bones*
Book Eleven—The Girl and the Black Christmas*
Book Twelve—The Girl and the Cursed Lake*
Book Thirteen—The Girl and The Unlucky 13*
Book Fourteen—The Girl and the Dragon's Island*

Season Three
Book Fifteen—The Girl in the Woods*
Book Sixteen —The Girl and the Midnight Murder*
Book Seventeen— The Girl and the Silent Night*
Book Eighteen — The Girl and the Last Sleepover*
Book Nineteen — The Girl and the 7 Deadly Sins*
Book Twenty — The Girl in Apartment 9*
Book Twenty-One — The Girl and the Twisted End*

Emma Griffin FBI Mysteries Retro - Limited Series
(Read as standalone or before Emma Griffin book 22)

Book One— The Girl in the Mist*
Book Two— The Girl on Hallow's Eve*
Book Three— The Girl and the Christmas Past*
Book Four— The Girl and the Winter Bones*
Book Five— The Girl on the Retreat*

Season Four

Book Twenty-Two — The Girl and the Deadly Secrets*
Book Twenty-Three — The Girl on the Road*
Book Twenty-Four — The Girl and the Unexpected Gifts*
Book Twenty-Five — The Girl and the Secret Passage*
Book Twenty-Six — The Girl and the Bride*
Book Twenty-Seven— The Girl in Her Cabin*
Book Twenty-Eight— The Girl Who Remembers

Season Five

Book Twenty-Nine — The Girl in the Dark

Ava James FBI Mysteries

Book One—The Woman at the Masked Gala*
Book Two—Ava James and the Forgotten Bones*
Book Three —The Couple Next Door*
Book Four — The Cabin on Willow Lake*
Book Five — The Lake House*
Book Six — The Ghost of Christmas*
Book Seven — The Rescue*
Book Eight — Murder in the Moonlight*
Book Nine — Behind the Mask*
Book Ten — The Invitation*
Book Eleven — The Girl in Hawaii*
Book Twelve — The Woman in the Window*
Book Thirteen — The Good Doctor

Dean Steele FBI Mysteries

Book One—The Woman in the Woods*
Book Two — The Last Survivors
Book Three — No Escape
Book Four — The Garden of Secrets
Book Five — The Killer Among Us
Book Six —The Convict
Book Seven —The Last Promise
Book Eight —Death by Midnight
Book Nine The — Woman in the Attic

ALSO BY
A.J. RIVERS & THOMAS YORK

Bella Walker FBI Mystery Series

Book One—The Girl in Paradise*
Book Two—Murder on the Sea*
Book Three —The Last Aloha*

Other Standalone Novels
Gone Woman
*Also available in audio

Made in the USA
Monee, IL
07 December 2024

72833541R00113